# I found your Diary

# I found your Diary

FRANCES THOMAS

Andersen Press • London

First published in 2004 by
Andersen Press Limited,
20 Vauxhall Bridge Road, London SWIV 2SA
www.andersenpress.co.uk



British Library Cataloguing in Publication Data available

ISBN 1 84270 347 1

Cover design by Sara Freeman

Typeset by FiSH Books, London WC1
Printed and bound in Great Britain by Bookmarque Ltd.,
Croydon, Surrey

# Chapter One

Dear Hannah,

I found your diary. I found it in a builder's skip just at the corner of my street. In among the usual skip rubbish – the dead cookers, broken window frames, the jagged bits of MDF, it was there in a plastic Sainsbury's bag. Other papers were spilling out from the bag; I'm not sure what exactly, but I think I remember letters and things. I didn't take any notice at the time, because it was just the diary that took my attention – such a nice big shiny black notebook. I thought it might be empty at first, which is why I picked it up – I need a new notebook.

But then I realised it wasn't empty – it was just full of your small neat quite beautiful handwriting. I felt a bit bad about taking it with me, to be honest. But then, I thought, it had been thrown away anyway, so there wasn't any harm. Perhaps you might want it back and I could get it to you.

But it was weird, that bag with your things. Almost as though someone was trying to get rid of you.

When I got home, I took it upstairs, feeling a bit guilty. I yelled down to Mum that I was home, and then shut my door and put my music on. I do this most days so she wasn't going to interrupt.

Then, still feeling like a real creep, I began to read.

I think you must have torn out the first page, because it suddenly began in the middle of a sentence...

...passed him in the corridor, and he stopped to say, 'That was a *great* essay, Hannah. Really good.' I didn't know what to say. I just sort of gawped like a fish. 'Oh, oh. Thank you.' He just smiled, that kind of sad smile that seems to go right through you, patted me lightly on the shoulder, and passed on clutching his usual bundle of files.

And I just thought, dumbly, a great essay. I'm not the one in the family to write great essays! That's for Grace, or Felix or Ruthie. But today it was me! Well!

For the rest of the day, I walked on air!

Nat has just phoned. He wants us to go out on Friday. But...I don't know. I'm not sure.

Anyway I said yes. But...

**Wednesday 19th September**

Something weird happened today. I didn't tell anyone so I'm telling my diary.

At least, I'm not sure if it even did happen!

I've just got out of the train at Notting Hill Gate. It's cold, and quite dark by the time I get there. There's that kind of misty gritty autumn air that gets in your throat, but I quite like that, just as I like all the windows lit up and crammed full of things for Christmas. Reminds you of being a little kid again, I suppose.

Well, I'm just starting to walk down the road in the direction of home, when I see something: a girl sitting in a heap in the doorway of W.H. Smith. She's wearing a black coat and a kind of purplish red scarf. I noticed because those are the colours I'm wearing, my old black cashmere coat from the Oxfam shop and the purply pretend pashmina Mum bought me for my last birthday.

The girl's sitting on the ground begging. She holds out a hand, and I catch a glimpse of her arm – it's thin as a skeleton, and all bruised. She lifts up her head – she has hair just like mine.

Then she turns, and I see her face, just for a second.

And it's my face.

Then the next moment, a surge of French schoolchildren rushes up the stairs from the train and suddenly they're all in front of me screaming and giggling. There's a great mass of them and they're everywhere. By the time they've passed, she's gone from the doorway.

It was all over in just a moment – really it takes much longer to write it than to have seen it.

And because I only saw her for a nanosecond, I'm not even absolutely a hundred per cent sure.

Actually now I come to think about it, I'm not sure at all.

In fact, no. Just a trick of the light.

Mum's calling me to supper.

What a performance that was! In the middle of Mum's amazing salmon-and-courgette pasta the phone rings and it's Grace, all the way from Kerala. She's met someone – his family are Indian, but he's studied in England, and she's in love! She's coming back next week anyway, but she couldn't wait to tell us. They want to get married. In January!! They are *desperately* in love, she says.

Mum goes into overdrive.

He's called Daniel.

I thought, how wonderful to have someone who loves you like that – so that it blocks out everything else.

That business about the girl in the doorway. It was just a trick of the light. The more I think about it. Really, I'm so dumb sometimes.

Probably he was just being kind when he said that about my essay.

Apparently they need help with the Senior play. I said I didn't know anything about lighting or anything. He said that was fine, but there were all sorts of other things – they're going to need a stage manager. And just at the moment there's a huge mound of photocopying. Anyway, Tasha and I volunteered, tomorrow after school.

I wonder where they're going to get married. Mum's in her element, kind of wound up but loving it. She keeps saying, I've got no time, no time, but you can tell she's happy. Dad just looks solemn but you know he's pleased though he never says anything – he wouldn't of course.

Grace said that she wants Ruthie and me to be bridesmaids. Funny, when I was little I used to long and long for someone to get married so I could be a bridesmaid, but they never did and I never was. But now – it's really quite scary.

I must go now and do my music.

I suppose tomorrow evening will be all right. I feel such a dork after what I said last year. I go cold whenever I think of it. *Are you a poet, Sir? You look like one!* Just because Tasha and Laura were there and I was showing off. All he must have thought was, what a loudmouth.

And actually, I didn't mean it like that. When he first came, I thought, with those dark eyes and that dark hair he did look like a poet, or at least what I imagined a poet to be like. The corduroy jacket for example, and the dark shirts. I thought it looked nice. Not very trendy, but I liked that.

Funny how you can be. At first I didn't really notice him. He didn't teach our year anyway. Miss Miller was doing her usual thing of putting us off English for life. (Now don't forget, girls, what have I told you about the correct use of prepositions? English is just like a tool, you must keep it sharp and polished! Now, don't let me hear anyone saying 'bored of' again. As you all know, it's 'bored *with*'.) Well, I was certainly bored of, with, by and from her.

Everyone who had him said, just wait till you get Mr Sinclair – he's really different. I didn't believe it at first. Didn't think he was even much to look at. Well, he isn't – he's not handsome, in a conventional way, I guess, plus he's so much older. But the things he told us about – Keats dying of TB, Milton going blind and making his daughters write things out for him, George Eliot being in love with a married man – made it all seem real, not just another thing to take an exam in.

**Thursday 20th September**

It was a foul day, right up until the evening. Then... Oh, I don't know.

But he made me feel grown up.

Tasha and I wandered over to the library after school. Tasha was in a foul mood – it was one of the things wrong with today. She's just had a row with her boyfriend, and we kept going through it back and forth. 'Do you think I should phone him, Han?' 'Yes, why don't you?' 'But he's such a selfish sod, if I phone him, he'll just think I'm running after him and people always run after him.' 'Don't phone him, then.' 'But suppose I don't phone, and he just thinks I'm sick of him and suppose he never phones back...'

I wanted to hit her and say, 'oh shut up'. Actually in the end I did say that, which was why she was sulking. 'I don't know why I agreed to do this,' she said. 'I'm tired. I want to go home.'

Mr Sinclair was in the library with a bundle of stuff. Letters to be printed out, collated and shoved in envelopes. Tasha stuck it for about five minutes and then stomped off. 'She's in a bad mood,' I explained. 'Boyfriend trouble.'

He smiled at me. 'It happens,' he said. 'You aren't going to desert me, I hope?'

''Course not.'

'Like a light in a storm. Good girl. Well, we'd best carry on. You man – or rather woman – the photocopier and I'll sort the pages.'

And then for a long time, we didn't say anything, just got on with it. Somehow it was nice. It wasn't like those times when you think, help, I've got to say something. We just worked together, as though we'd done it for years.

And then he said something really amazing. He said, 'You have the gift of repose, Hannah. It's a wonderful thing.'

I went bright red. 'What do you mean?'

'I mean, you can be yourself without feeling that you have to fill every gap with jabber. Not many people of your age can manage that.'

Well, I didn't say that for the last few minutes I'd actually been trying to think of something brilliant to say, like, Have you seen that new play at the National? Or the exhibition at the Tate? Which I thought would be the way Mum would have managed the silence. But I hadn't done anything interesting and I couldn't think. Was that repose? I don't know. But I liked the way he said it.

Of course I went on to spoil it by jabbering. 'But that's only because when I do talk it's so stupid.'

'Don't knock yourself, Hannah. You're a highly intelligent girl, with some rare qualities.'

Well. Wow.

Anyway we'd finished by then. He offered to drive me to the bus stop. And I wanted him to, but it seemed silly to want it. After all, it was only about half past five by this time. So I said no.

And then he went home and then I went home.

**Friday 21st September**

Met Nat this evening as arranged. He was waiting outside Pizza Express, at 8.30. The conversation went like this:

(Him) Want a pizza?

(Me) I'm not fussed.

(Him) Well, what do you want to do?

(Me) I don't know. You think of something.

(Him) I don't know.

The rest of the evening was pretty much the same. We went to the pub, and couldn't hear each other talking over the noise. We walked up and down the High Street. He decided he was hungry after all, so he went for this big disgusting doner. We walked back through the churchyard and he got me into a corner and tried to have a good grope. But he stunk of kebab and so I pushed him away and said I'd got my period and didn't feel like it. Sometimes I think boys will believe anything. He was in a strop for the rest of the walk home, just grunted, 'See ya,' on the doorstep and stomped off.

A few months ago we used to have a lot to say to each other. He used to make me laugh. I don't know what's gone wrong. But I think maybe I won't bother seeing him again.

**Saturday 22nd September**

I can't wait to see Grace next weekend. Mum's planning this special lunch. And Dad is fairly relaxed, for him. I know Grace is his favourite, and that's all right, it is really. And she does have repose. She doesn't get anxious or strung up over things.

**Monday 24th September**

Like a real dork I said to Tasha about being a bridesmaid. 'Ooh,' she said. 'Just see you all in pink!'

I said Grace won't want those sorts of bridesmaids.

And she said, yes, she will, because everyone wants their bridesmaids to look really ugly, so they'll look gorgeous by contrast. She says everyone will be saying that I look like a fat frump. I know she's in a bad mood, but still . . .

I got on the scales this evening and I was almost nine stone! I was gobsmacked. I really will be a fat frump!

**Tuesday 25th September**

He walked right past me in the corridor today without even a smile. Obviously I'm just a stupid schoolgirl to him.

Grace emailed us – they're leaving India on Saturday and she and Daniel are coming to lunch on Sunday. She told us more about Daniel – he's an Indian Catholic apparently so Dad will be pleased. He's a Human Rights lawyer and he's twenty-six years old. They want to get married in the Oratory if they can, which sounds a bit posh for us! But one of his uncles knows the priests there, and it will be nice if his parents come over, for the wedding to be somewhere really special.

If I had someone I really loved, I'd just like to sneak out one morning in a floaty dress and sandals and just get married quietly in a registry office, have lunch in the pub and then go back and tell everyone. I don't know why, this has always been my idea of the perfect wedding – just a private moment.

But of course you'll upset your parents. And Dad will be upset if I don't get married in church anyway. I wish I could be a better Catholic – I wish I could be a Catholic at all – for him, but I'm not. I can't see the point of God, to be honest. There are such foul things in the world – it's really better to think there's no God at all rather than one who just lets these things happen.

I've had this conversation with Dad but we never get anywhere and he just looks hurt. You can't make yourself believe. Mum says it doesn't matter, but I know he must feel I'm going to Hell.

But being Dad, he doesn't say anything.

Anyway, I can do something about being a fat frump! Started today. Didn't have seconds of lasagne and no pudding.

# Chapter Two

Actually, Hannah, I'm a bit worried about you. I mean, don't get me wrong but that English teacher sounds well weird. And I definitely think you should ditch Tasha. What is it with you girls? Luke, who I guess is my 'best friend' – though I've never called him that in my life – and I argue all the time, but we don't bitch at each other like you seem to. Nearly nine stone doesn't sound enormous to me, either. I suppose it depends on how tall you are, and I kind of see you as quite tall, I don't know why. And long dark hair. Am I right?

Oh, this is getting a bit pervy. Let's go and see what delights Mum's got for supper tonight.

I meant to say it to Mum, that I'd found this girl's diary, and I was only hanging on to it until I could find out who she was and give it back to her.

The moment was there, but somehow I didn't say it.

Which means that now it's turned into a secret and it's going to get harder to say with every minute.

Oh hell. Well, just as soon as I find out who you are, I'll stop reading your diary, Hannah, I promise.

Anyway, I can't read any more for the moment as I've arranged to meet Cara. Just a pizza and maybe a drink afterwards. Not a late night or anything.

I said to Cara over my peperoni with extra extra cheese, 'How much do you weigh, Cara?'

She burst out laughing. 'What sort of a question is that? You are seriously weird, Tom Palmer, did you know that?'

'I just wanted to know, that's all.'

'You trying to tell me I'm too fat?'

'No, 'course not. You look great. But it's just . . . I heard these girls talking, and one of them said nine stone. Is that huge?'

'Depends how tall you are, I guess. Tom, what is this?'

'Like I said. Just curious.'

The nice thing about Cara is she never gets paranoid like some girls do. I mean, you can't insult her or anything – you wouldn't want to – but she's not all touchy. She's not a great looker, but she always looks nice. Her dad's black and her mum's white. Her mum has this huge nose and big teeth, and Cara's teeth are a bit big, but then she has this nice golden skin and quite groovy hair, which she does bother about – it's the one thing she fusses over. At the moment, it's in sort of short dreadlocks. I just like her. We have a good time together.

And when she'd got over laughing at what I'd asked her, she said, 'Well, I'm just over nine stone at the moment. I could lose half a stone really. But nine stone isn't enormous unless you're tiny. Does that answer your question, weird person?'

'Yes, I guess. Do you want ice-cream?'

'What, after you asking me how much I weigh? You must be joking. Let's go and see if there's anyone in the Gladstone.'

The Gladstone is where some of the kids from our school hang out. The downside is they've got all fussed about underage drinking, so you can't sneak a pint there. But there's usually quite a decent crowd there, even in the middle of the week, so Cara and I often end up there.

When I get back home, it's quite late. I play some music with my headphones on, but soon I'm asleep.

I keep thinking about Hannah and her diary, though. I really ought to get it back to her somehow.

Of course, there were other things of hers in that builder's skip. Maybe I could get her address from a letter or something. Perhaps she was mugged in the street. Or maybe her mum just threw out a load of stuff without asking, the way my mum does sometimes – there was that time when I used to collect Pokémon cards where she threw out half my collection just thinking they were bits of old paper. I've only just got round to forgiving her for that.

I mooch around a bit after school with Luke and some of the others. Still, it's not late when I'm getting off the bus at the corner.

There's still a skip there.

But it's empty. They've taken the old one away, and it's a new one.

Oh hell. Too late now. Whatever else there was of hers is on its way to a landfill somewhere. I missed my chance to rescue her things.

So I've made a big sandwich – peanut butter, Hellman's and lettuce, grabbed a can of cherry Coke, turned up my music and settled down for another go at Hannah's diary. I'm still looking for clues about her. As soon as I find something, I'll stop reading and take it back to her...

**Sunday 30th September**

Mum said this was a 'red-letter day' for our family – the first marriage! Grace brought Daniel round and he is really sweet. I'd thought he was going to be tall, but he wasn't that tall. Good-looking, though. And just so polite and dignified in that way Indian people are. He said he was 'privileged' to meet Mum and Dad, and it was a real honour to know Grace. He talks like that – in someone else you might want to take the mick, but not with him. And he just *adores* Grace – you can tell by the way he looks at her across the table. They want to get married soon because he's about to take on a new job in a new city and he wants Grace to be there with him. They're going to get married here, and then go back to India, for the next few years anyway.

Grace was wearing a sari and it looked beautiful on her. She's going to get married in a traditional European wedding dress, though. She said she fancied a kind of 'column' of white silk. And me and Ruth will be bridesmaids, along with two of Daniel's sisters. She said she thought of pink, but a deep pink, not like Tasha's idea. She said she wasn't going to make us look like pink meringues, but the dresses would be straight and simple.

I asked about Daniel's sisters. She said they're really tiny – she said when you take one of their hands it's like taking hold of a little bird, all fragile and dainty.

I was a bit piggy at lunchtime – perhaps it was all the excitement. I had seconds of the Thai chicken salad, and I even had a slice of Mum's special chocolate-and-cream celebration cake.

**Tuesday 2nd October**

It's a rehearsal Thursday night and I promised Mr Sinclair I'd help. Tasha, we've both decided, is rubbish! No point in even asking her.

**Thursday 4th October**

The rehearsal went on forever. Millie Simpson is hopeless as Viola. I bet he regrets asking her. Sami is quite good as Orsino. Julia thinks just showing off will do for Malvolio.

Millie has this wonderful speech, and she completely screwed it up:

*Make me a willow cabin at your gate*
*And call upon my soul within the house...*

When I listened to her, I really wished I'd gone for

those auditions, exams or no exams.

And afterwards there was all this mess to clear up and everyone just sort of vanished. He turned to me with a look. The hall was littered with furniture and plastic bags. They'd even left crisp packets and plastic bottles.

'Don't worry, Sir,' I said. 'I'll help you.'

'I wish you wouldn't *Sir* me,' he said. 'I can't get my head round Sir.'

'Why not?'

He smiled, his sad-Pierrot smile. 'One of the things they don't tell you, Hannah, about growing up is that you never really feel you've made it. I might look old and wrinkly to you, but inside I don't feel any different from the lumpish schoolboy I used to be. Does that sound very foolish?'

'But you're not old and wrinkly,' I say.

'Nice of you to say so, but you can't argue with your mirror in the morning.'

I don't know exactly how old he is – somewhere over forty, I guess. I know his son and daughter aren't that much younger than me. I've seen his wife. She doesn't smile much. I don't know what she does.

But he really doesn't look old! I tell him so again.

Then he says something that surprises and embarrasses me too. 'I'll always be grateful for something you said, Hannah.'

'What was that, Sir?'

'Couldn't we manage *Geoffrey*? Try it. Just when

we're working together like this, I mean. Go on, just give it a whirl. It won't bite.'

I try it. 'What was it that I said, Geoffrey?' I giggle. It sounds dead cheeky.

'You told me I looked like a poet.'

'Oh, Sir! I mean . . . ' I feel myself blushing. Why remember that stupid thing?

'Because when I was young like you, and uncorrupted, I used to want to be a poet, more than anything else. Used to write long screeds, no capital letters and no grammar. They were terrible. But a few people told me I had promise. If only I'd stuck it out. But I never stuck it out.'

'Why not?'

'Because . . . Oh I don't know. Life got in the way. And then I married and had the kids. And you feel a little stupid writing odes to the moon when you've got gas bills to pay and you're worried about whether it's rising damp or not in the kitchen . . . '

'But you still could. Be a poet, I mean.'

'I could, of course I could. Forget it, Hannah. I'm just a dreamer. We're a hopeless crew, we middle-aged dreamers.'

'But you should stop saying middle-aged.'

'Nevertheless. Anyway, forget it. I'm just feeling sorry for myself.'

'Not at all! And I like talking to you.'

'It's lovely talking to you, Hannah. And I think that's half my trouble, no one to talk to.'

'But your . . . ' I want to say *your wife*, but I don't quite dare to. So instead, I say 'your children. Can't you talk to them?'

But then he sort of answers the question I've been wondering about.

'I'm a bit of a cuckoo in the nest at home, I'm afraid. They all think I'm daft as a brush. All into health and fitness and athletics, thanks to Jenny. She loves jogging and going to the gym. And Olivia's a runner, and Joe plays basketball. And there's stupid old Dad just reads poetry.'

I notice that he's named his daughter after the play we're doing . . .

*Halloo your name to the reverberate hills,*
*And make the babbling gossip of the air*
*Cry out, 'Olivia'.*

He must have wanted someone like himself, instead of a big, sporty girl. A kind of shiver runs down my spine. I've never had a conversation like this with anyone before. I want to stay for ever, talking, but also I want to run away. I don't know what to do.

He must have seen this too, for he suddenly laughs. 'Listen to us, eh, Hannah! Whatever would people think? Come on, we've both got homes to go to.'

And so we say goodbye, outside the hall, and I walk to the bus stop. My head feels light and my feet feel like lead. I don't know what's happening.

It's dark now, and raw. Lights glitter and shimmer on the road. Windows are lit up, and people look so safe and enclosed inside them, like jewels in golden jewel cases, while I'm out in the cold.

Then a bus draws up. I put my hand up and rush to get on it, but it's full. It just slows down a fraction and drives off, the windows lit up and bulging with people. They all seem to look at me standing at the bus stop, as if they pity me.

And then I see *her* again, her face pressed to the glass. She doesn't smile, and she's thin and pale and there are great bruised shadows under her eyes.

But her face . . .

**Saturday 6th October**

There was no reason why he should have talked to me yesterday. After all, it meant nothing to him, it can't have meant what it meant to me.

But when he just passed in the corridor without even a look. I felt so stupid. And so mean expecting more.

**Sunday 7th October**

I pleased Dad by going to church with him. It was quite boring, and that priest who gives me the creeps gave a horrible sermon about good thoughts. He said, it wasn't enough just to do good things for charity – he said that was typically non-Catholic, just to immerse yourself in charities, and assume you're doing yourself and the world some good. He said the only way the world will change is if people become good, inside. And you can't do that on your own, only with God's help. I suppose Dad really does believe in God. He didn't say much in the car driving home, but I think he was glad I went. Though I'm not sure why I did.

Grace came round in the afternoon, with wedding plans. It's all happening so fast! Mum's phoning round caterers. Grace's found this wedding shop in Fulham, and has already decided on her dress. We're going to have the bridesmaids' dresses made there too so Ruthie and I are going to go in and be measured next Saturday. Daniel's sisters will just have to email their measurements. You can't imagine how much work goes into planning a wedding. Not to mention the cake and the flowers and the invitations!

**Monday 8th October**

He must be cross with me. We had English and he never spoke. I answered a question once and he sounded quite cross. Come on, Hannah, he said, you must remember what I told you all about the French Revolution the other day. That's what Wordsworth's talking about in this poem!

Then he addresses all of us. Come on, you dozy crew! Wake up!

**Wednesday 10th October**

The rehearsal was totally frantic, and he was in a foul mood, shouting at everyone. He made Millie cry. Lou Ward forgot her lines. Dorcas and Kate as Sir Toby and Andrew Aguecheek are just pathetic.

I should have left it, but I couldn't. I said, 'Are you

cross with me, Sir?' Because he had been. Foul.

And he spun round, clutching his copy of the play, and just said, without a smile or anything, 'You, Hannah? No, I'm not cross with you.'

And that was it. I didn't get a chance to talk to him again.

**Saturday 13th October**

Oh my God, we've just been for our measurements. Mum took me and Ruthie. It's a hushed, white shop with gilt chairs and a rail of white dresses like clouds. They are so beautiful. There was a girl there just trying on her dress. She had golden hair, polished golden skin, and she wore this shimmer of white. It looked just gorgeous. Even Mum noticed.

The girl hardly smiled. She said to the designer, 'Let's lower that line a little bit, and pull in the seam on the hip, and adjust the neckline.' Didn't ask. *Said.*

All as serious as if she were at church, taking the Blessed Sacrament, as Dad calls it. But it will be her day of days, so why not?

*My heart is gladder than all these,*
*Because my love is come to me…*

The designer is called Lois. She doesn't smile much either. She remembered Grace. Very pretty girl, she said. Then she looked at me, and said, well, let's measure you up.

And I was mortified. I'm still a size twelve!!! I

thought after all last week's effort it would at least have gone down to a ten. Ruthie will look all right in hers – after all she's only twelve and her bits haven't started to bulge yet.

When Mum showed her Daniel's sisters' measurements Lois looked really impressed. 'But they're tiny!' she said. 'They'll only need an eight or a ten.'

And she looked at me again.

I had my mobile off in the shop of course and afterwards I found Nat had been phoning and texting like mad. He wants me to go out tonight. But I said I wanted an early night.

I don't know why it is, but boys of my own age just seem so young and crude now. They have no conversation. All they care about is football and getting inside your pants. Maybe girls grow up faster. I don't know.

Anyway, I'm staying home tonight.

Well, thanks a bunch, Hannah. Did it never occur to you that these wonderful sophisticated older men, with absolutely no interest in football or your underwear and so great at *conversation* also started off as spotty louts? Did it also never occur to you that maybe some of these old guys aren't quite so squeaky-clean as you seem to think?

Get real, Hannah.

# Chapter Three

**Monday 15th October**

So today The Diet starts properly! I got it off to a good start by not having any breakfast. But I hadn't realised I'd be so hungry by lunchtime. Anyway, I was really good at lunch. I only had half my sandwiches and gave the other half to Candy Birch who is a fat cow and will eat anything.

This evening I was so ravenous that I could hardly think straight. But I drank heaps of water, and didn't make too much of a pig of myself this evening. I said to Mum we ought to have fresh fruit instead of puddings as it's better for us, and she agreed.

I intend to be size ten by Christmas.

Everyone was teasing me today. 'Look, Hannah, there goes your boyfriend! Say hallo to lover-boy!' I suppose I have been banging on about him a bit – I just can't help myself. But I must shut up about it. Everybody is being very childish about it, really.

**Tuesday 16th October**

It's cold and misty today – I love this weather, though no one else in the family does.

I came home through Kensington High Street because

I wanted to look for shoes. Couldn't see any I liked.

But – I thought I saw *her* again, just going into the station. It was probably just a trick of the light.

No breakfast today, either. I didn't feel nearly so bad today. The thing is to get used to it and your stomach will shrink.

**Wednesday 17th October**

Oh my God. I feel as though I'm floating.

It was lunchtime. I'd had my sandwiches, and I'd just been to the loo. I was making my way to the sixth form common room, going by the back stairway. Suddenly he was there, clutching his usual bundle of stuff. I said, 'Hallo, Sir', and he said, 'Hallo, Hannah', and he seemed about to go on, then he stopped and called me back.

'Hannah?'

'Yes, Sir?'

'Look, this is probably daft of me, but . . . ' And for a moment, it looked as if he were really worried about asking me, just as I'd be worried about asking him. I felt dead flattered.

'Do you by any chance like opera, Hannah?'

Well, sort of. Dad dragged me once to *The Magic Flute* when I was little, and though the music was nice it just seemed to go on and on. And there was that time in Italy a couple of years ago where we saw *Il Trovatore*, which I thought was the silliest story ever.

Still, since I started doing the clarinet, though I'm not

good at it, like Felix is, I'm a bit better informed about music, so I said, yes, I guess I do.

'The thing is, I've got two tickets for *Madame Butterfly*, this Friday at the Coliseum. Jenny really doesn't want to go. She said, why don't you take one of those clever sixth formers you're always telling me about?'

'Your wife said that?'

'I told you, Hannah, she'll just about tolerate the theatre if it's a nice musical, but opera's her idea of hell. You'd be doing us both a favour, really.'

I slowly process this. He's asking me to go out with him. He likes me enough for that.

I said, yes, I'd love to come.

He said, great, so we'd meet up in the foyer at about seven.

And then he said, 'Oh and Hannah?'

'Yes, Sir?'

'People might not . . . So you know . . . '

Yes, I knew what he meant. Of course I wouldn't tell anyone. They'd only get the wrong end of the stick.

Nat phoned this evening. He had these plans to go clubbing on Saturday. He knows I'm not a clubbing girl. Anyway, I'd been thinking about this for a bit. I said, 'Look, Nat, I'm sorry, but I don't think this is working out.'

He said, 'What are you on about?'

I said, 'This. Us going out.'

He said, 'What are you trying to say?'

'I'm not *trying* to say anything. I'm saying I think we should call it a day.'

'Call it a day? You mean stop seeing each other?' Well, full marks for deduction, Nat.

'Yes, I guess. I mean, you have to admit, it isn't as much fun as it was.'

'Only because you've been such a grouchy cow lately.'

Now that's not true. Trust him to blame me. Typical boy.

I said, 'I'm sorry, Nat. It's not working out, whatever you say. We may as well pack it in.'

And he goes, 'But I don't understand.'

And then, I feel really bad. He starts crying down the phone. He says he really loves me and he had no idea and all that...

I didn't know he felt as strongly as that. But it can't be helped. I don't want him around. I don't want him all over me. I don't want to have to listen to him boring on about football and what his daft mates at school said and things on telly.

I did like him once. When we first went out, I was quite struck, for a bit. But it's over now.

He said, 'Is there somebody else?' And of course I said no.

Nobody would understand. They'd think it was just a schoolgirl crush. But I know I'm better than that, and it isn't, it really isn't.

They say there are some people who have just one big love in their lives. Could I be one of them?

And – oh – could *he*? Shut up, Hannah, you daft cow.

He's being nice enough to take you to the opera, let that be enough for you.

Now all I have to do is to wait until Friday.

I'm going to wear my new violet-blue top and that floaty black skirt, and my black ankle-strap shoes. I don't want to look too tarted-up, but I don't want to look like a schoolgirl either. With any luck I should be able to lose a couple of pounds by Friday, no problem.

Oh, I don't know. This is all making me feel a bit of a creep. Like one of those stalkers. I still haven't found out where she lives or anything. I should stop reading.

It's one o'clock in the morning. Mum's fast asleep. We had a really nice evening, nothing special, but I'm feeling good. Cara came round and Mum said, 'Oh sod it, I don't feel like cooking for you lot this evening.' So we sent off for Chinese take-away, masses of noodles and sweet-and-sour, and Peking duck with those little pancakes. We all gorged and gorged till we were stuffed, then we watched 'ER' followed by this really trash programme about Hollywood sex scandals. I thought it was bollocks, but the women loved it.

Then afterwards, Mum, who can be tactful at times, said she was exhausted and went off to bed, leaving me and Cara in the living room.

Well, I guess, like Nat, I must have stunk of take-away, but Cara wasn't being fussed about it. I really like her.

Later on I walked her home, and now I'm back here.

I should be thinking of Cara, but for some reason all I can think of is Hannah. Somehow, I can't imagine her having a nice relaxed evening like the one I've just had; what with her mother who seems to spend all her time cooking and her father who thinks she's going to hell, and her sisters and her brother who are all cleverer than she is. I wonder how they spend their evenings. Not watching rubbish TV, I bet.

I feel kind of sorry for Nat. Then part of me starts thinking, all the more room for you to get on in there, Tom.

Which is stupid, because she's got the hots for this bloke old enough to be my father and hers too.

Oh hell.

I can't believe she's left so few clues about herself. There's no hint about where she lives, or where she goes to school. It sounds like an all girls' school, since there don't seem to be any blokes around apart from Mr Perv. And I get the impression it's one of these posh private schools, too. Her dad's a Catholic, but I don't know what he does, or her mum. Her sister's been working in India and is about to have a posh wedding. She talks about Notting Hill Gate and Kensington High Street, so I guess it's sort of local. But I don't know.

Oh this is stupid. I'm not going to read any more of this. I'll shove it in a drawer and forget it. That's what I'll do.

# Chapter Four

. . . so I do, for a few days, anyway. But I can't help wondering what's been happening to her. So here I am again. Mum thinks I'm doing homework. But I've turned my sounds up high, though I don't imagine they're Hannah's scene at all and here I am stretched out on the bed, starting to read again . . .

**Thursday 18th October**

I'm trying not to think about it, but it's useless. My head's going round and round. I wish I knew more about *Madame Butterfly*. I looked it up in our *Dictionary of Opera* – she's Japanese and she marries an American who deserts her and marries someone else. At the end she kills herself because – hey – it's opera. But I don't think I'll be able to hold an intelligent conversation about it. Grace would be able to say things like, 'I do admire the terribly courageous contrapuntal use of the string section in the third act.' But all I can manage is 'nice' or 'boring'. I'm terrified he'll find out just how dumb I really am.

One good thing though – I managed it without lying. Well not really lying. I said to Mum that I was off to the opera with some people – that our English teacher had got hold of some tickets. Well, all of that is true if you pick it to pieces. I don't think Mum noticed anyway. She's going to be away Friday and Saturday anyway at some conference. Dad of course, bless him, never notices anything.

Ruthie – eagle-eyes – just might spot it if I'm acting strange, so I'll have to be very careful.

He's right of course. People wouldn't understand. They'd think he was just a dirty old man and I was a silly schoolgirl. Well, I'm that all right. But he isn't.

I remember him saying a few weeks ago, when we were doing Keats, that Keats thought that the most important thing in life was 'the holiness of the heart's affections'. He said that what Keats meant was that we should trust our instincts of love, because they're purer and better than anything else we have or do.

Well I trust mine.

**Friday 19th October**

Just a note. I have to leave the house in ten minutes, but it's too early yet. I spent ages in the bathroom, but I often do so Ruth didn't get too suspicious.

I think I've lost two pounds. Well, if I stand carefully on the scales.

Will I need to put more lipstick on on the bus? Will my hair get mussed up? I'm so nervous I keep wanting to pee.

I'm going now. Oh God.

*

**Later**

I can't believe I was so scared. It was the most wonderful evening of my life. I won't forget any of it, ever, but I'll try and write all of it down anyway. Maybe when I'm a little old lady, I'll take this down from the shelf and read it.

Okay. Try to describe it.

It's freezing cold outside, with this drizzling misty icy rain, so in spite of having spent so much time glamming myself up, I set off wrapped up completely in my big black coat and a scarf round my head. But I don't have to wait long for the bus and soon I'm upstairs on the top deck in a fug of wet wool and musty old people. They all look dazed and bored, while I'm thinking to myself, My life is just beginning – tonight my life is beginning!

We arranged to meet at seven, and I'm there a bit early. But before I start wondering what I'm going to do, I see *him*, already there.

For just a nanosecond, he looks just like anyone else's dad, standing there with his head down and his hands in his pockets, looking restless, even a little nervous. Then he looks up, sees me, gives a big smile and my heart jumps in the air.

The foyer is crowded with people, but I don't take much notice of them, as he takes my arm and ushers me upstairs to the circle where our seats are. He's already bought me a programme which he hands me with a smile. He says that he's seen *Madame Butterfly* a few times before but not for ages, so he's really looking forward to it. Most of the other people here seem very old, even older than he is, all draped in dowdy shawls and bad shiny jackets. He's wearing a dark jacket I haven't seen before, and quite a surprising tie with violet splashes. He nods at my top. 'We match, Hannah.' We do. I like that.

He ushers me into my seat and then fusses about whether my view is blocked by the man in front. He asks if I'm comfortable, not too hot, if I've already eaten. Actually I completely forgot to eat, but I'm not at all hungry. I feel myself replying a bit stupidly to all the things he asks, so in a way I'm glad when the conductor comes on, the lights dim, and the music starts.

At first, I can't concentrate on anything going on onstage where two blokes are singing away. All I can think of is that he's sitting next to me. I'm aware of his smell – a clean smell of soap and some sort of lemony cologne, but there's also a kind of shabby smell coming off his jacket as though he hasn't worn it for a long time. It's somehow very different from sitting next to Nat at the cinema, though I don't quite know why. Sometimes our elbows brush each other on the armrest. The first few times this happens, we snatch our arms away, but then as things settle down, I realise that I can feel the pressure of his arm against mine, and he's not taking it away.

Then in spite of myself I get carried away by the story. There seems to be some sort of arranged marriage going on, and lots of Japanese-ish people swirl about. Butterfly herself is a bit old for the job, not to say a little hefty, and doesn't look remotely Eastern, but it doesn't matter. Her American husband looks as though he's going to be really nice to her, they have this beautiful love scene, and then you know they're just off to bed and the curtain comes down.

This is where the interval comes. We join the surge out of the auditorium. He finds a space by the wall and propels me there. I love the way older men know their way about and think about you. Imagine it ever occurring to Nat to find a quiet place for me to stand.

He smiles at me. 'You like?'

'Oh yes! I like.'

'Can I get you a drink?'

I don't want to put him in a spot by asking for alcohol so I ask for fizzy water. Then I wish I hadn't as I realise I'll lose ten minutes of his company as he fights his way to the bar. However, eventually he comes back with wine for himself and water for me. He says, 'I envy you, you know. I'd really love to be seeing all these things for the first time again. You can't ever quite recapture that magic.'

It's truer than he knows. There'll never be magic like this again, not for me. And for the last ten minutes of the interval, we seem to find our voices, and we're just chatting away. Afterwards I'm embarrassed because I've been yakking. I should have been quieter and more mysterious, I guess. But too late.

Anyway soon we're back in our seats for the second and third acts.

When the curtain goes up, you're aware that time has passed, that Butterfly and her servant are now very poor and everything's in rags. Her American seems to have buggered off. But she looks out of the window and sings this heartbreaking song about how one fine day she'll be looking out, and she'll see this ship on the horizon and it'll be him coming home to her.

Of course you know she's wrong. How is it that everyone else can see that when she can't? But that's opera for you, I guess. Then amazingly, it seems to be coming true. There is a ship and he's on it. What she doesn't know is he's also brought his new American wife, because in his eyes the Japanese marriage doesn't really count.

Then – oh, it just gets sadder and sadder. There's such a long bit where there's no sound except all the Japanese women humming softly. There were tears rolling down my cheeks at the end, when she realises he doesn't love her, never really loved her and was just using her. And she kills herself.

And suddenly it's over and the lights blaze on and there am I sitting with tears on my face and God only knows what it's done to my mascara, while all around these ugly old people start banging on about the contrapuntal strings in the third act.

I feel so embarrassed. The old dears are standing up all around us and we have to move. And as we're moving through the press of people, he puts a hand on my shoulder and whispers in my ear, 'Don't worry. I always cry at that bit too.' He gives my shoulder a comforting squeeze and I feel much better again.

And then all too soon, we're out in the street. We're hit by a surge of icy cold wind, but somehow it doesn't make me feel cold. I imagine I'm red as a beetroot all over by now. There are hordes and hordes of people. Again, he's pushing me through so confidently. I wonder if he's going to suggest going for a drink or something, but he says, 'Well, I guess we better get you home.'

He says he'll take me home on the bus, and then get the Tube back himself, so we set off towards Oxford Street. The streets are full of people, old people going home and young people coming out. He knows some fiendish short cuts through back streets, but then as we turn a corner we meet a wave of noise. There's this big group of kids, all about my age, only they're completely out of their skulls. They surge round the corner, yelling and shouting and blocking the pavement. We have to step into the gutter, even though one of them is being noisily sick. His arm tightens around my shoulder and I can hear him tutting. Then a second wave of them breaks around us, arms linked and singing raucously. In spite of the cold most of them are skimpily dressed.

And then, in the second group, I see *her*. She has both arms flung round two blokes and her mouth is wide open in a contemptuous chant. She's wearing a violet-blue top and a black skirt, torn tights and teetery shoes. Her arms are blotchy and bruised, her face is spotty. She has rings in her lip and her nose.

For a long second our eyes meet.

Then it's all over and he's pulled me away, and we've turned the corner into another quieter street. I wonder if he saw what I did, but his face is intent on getting us through the crowd, and I don't think he looked from left to right.

We stop, and he stands back, his arms still on my shoulders and looks into my eyes. 'You all right, Hannah?'

I nod; I can't say anything.

He gives me a hug, and I feel his jacket against my cheek. I want to clutch him, and bury myself in his warmth. But we quickly pull apart, and he says, 'Young people like that. I just can't understand why they behave that way. What pleasure can there possibly be in it for them?'

I manage to shake my head in agreement. I suppose he thinks I was frightened by them being so drunk. He pulls my arm through his and we walk quickly and in silence through the dark streets. Anyone seeing us must just think it's a daughter out with her dad.

The bus journey's great, though. I'm able to forget what I've just seen, and we talk away once more. He tells me about when he was at school – an old-style boys' grammar school somewhere in Surrey – how he was an only son and his parents had such great aspirations for him. How hard it was for him. He says, 'I often wonder what they'd think if they could see me now.'

I say, 'I'm sure they'd be very happy.'

He says, 'I wonder about that, Hannah. Sometimes I–

think that nothing I could have achieved would have been good enough for them.'

I say, 'I feel a bit the same about my parents.'

'I met your mother last parents' day. I thought she was charming.'

'Oh she is. And clever. And successful. That's the trouble.'

'They can have nothing to be dissatisfied with about *you*, Hannah.'

Well, there are plenty of things, actually. But it's nice to hear him say it.

And then the bus journey is over. We get off at Holland Park Station and set off through the streets. And at the corner of the Square, he stops, pulls me to him, and just so briefly, kisses me on the lips. 'I'll watch you to your front door,' is all he says. 'Off you go now.'

'Goodbye . . . ' I'm still too shy to use his name, so I just say goodbye.

He doesn't say anything, just gives his sad little smile. I set off. At the gate I turn, and he's standing there, a huddled shape under the street lamp. He gives me a little wave and then turns and strides quickly off.

I let myself into the house. There's no one about. I can hear Dad listening to music from the front room, and Ruth seems to have gone to bed.

I call out, 'Goodnight', and then I'm upstairs and in the silence and privacy of my room. I shut the door, take a deep breath, and let the thoughts of everything that's happened to me tonight rush over me in a glorious wave.

# Chapter Five

**Sunday 21st October**
Sometimes you just want to stop the clock, and keep things just as they are for ever, like that film where he went over and over the same weekend time after time. Because I just want my night at the opera to go on happening for ever.

The weekend is rather tricky. Grace's here and far from the wedding being wonderful, everyone's having rows. Mum and Dad are quibbling over what it's going to cost. Mum wants to go for a cheaper caterer, Grace wants this amazing firm that her best friend had. Grace wants everything of the best, flowers, invitations, music. Mum and Dad niggle. Dad gets quite angry.

Felix is down from Oxford and he's in a tricky mood, too, I don't know why. He teases Grace and he teases me all the time, only it doesn't seem to be friendly teasing. I guess he's got problems of some sort and is taking them out on us.

But the result is, that it's a pretty miserable weekend. And now Grace has gone back to her flat, Felix is back in Oxford, Ruthie is being a pain, but I've shut the door, and got a CD of *Madame Butterfly* playing in my headphones. I try to bring back Friday night, and sometimes hearing the music almost does, and then it goes again. I keep thinking horrible thoughts – suppose he's killed in a car accident, then nobody will ever know that I loved him. It'll all vanish into the air. I feel happy, and sick, and anxious all together.

I wish tomorrow was here. I can't wait to see him again.

**Tuesday 30th October**
But things never turn out like you think. For the last week he's barely taken any notice of me. We've had English a couple of times, and he's stood there, talking to us, but it's as though I don't exist. Once I do manage to get him in the corridor, and I say, 'I loved it, the other night. Thank you so much.' And he turns and looks down at me, as if I'd said no more than, That was a good lesson, Sir, and he goes, 'Good. Good. Well done,' and walks off. I feel stupid, and small.

**Friday 2nd November**
Which I still do. We've had two rehearsals – only a week left now, so everything is very busy and frantic, he's rushing around, being quite bad-tempered, to tell the truth.

One nice thing, though, is that people keep coming up to me and saying, 'Have you lost weight, Hannah? You look really great.'

So I'm good at something, anyway.

**Saturday 3rd November**
A letter from Nat this morning. Poor Nat – he's such a

rubbish writer. It looked as though a mad centipede had rushed around on the page. He says he still loves me and wants me to give him another chance. But another chance for what? There's nothing wrong with Nat. It's just that he isn't *him.* I don't think I could ever go back to boys of my own age now. But if Geoffrey isn't talking to me, where does that leave me?

Oh it's all such a mess.

Anyway I've been really good so far. This morning for breakfast I had two rice cakes with a smear of marmite. They taste disgusting but they're only 28 calories each. I'll try and cut it down to one. For lunch I just had a low-fat yoghurt. Even though I'm starving I'm not going to eat anything until tonight – Mum's making chicken with rice and as long as I don't eat the skin, I should be all right.

Grace asked if I'd find two poems to read at the wedding – they've got to be about love but also suitable for a church, so nothing too sexy. She says everyone goes for Shakespeare's sonnets, so she wants something different. I'm supposed to be this great expert on English literature, what with everyone else being into law and economics, so I have to be the one to find them. I've no idea what to go for.

**Wednesday 7th November**

It's the play on Thursday and Friday – it's going to be frantic. Half the costumes aren't ready and Andrew Aguecheek has 'flu. I have to rush down the road to some music studio to pick up a lute that he's hired. It's all rush rush rush and panic stations.

I caught a glimpse of myself in the cloakroom mirror – I looked such a lump. How can they keep saying I'm thin?

**Thursday 8th November**
I'm so sick of this wretched play. It seems to take up all his energy – it's as though I've lost him.

**Friday 9th November**
Well, they do say it'll be all right on the night, and actually it was, in spite of the disaster of dress rehearsal. How Millie could say she knew her lines! But then, it was a triumph, in the end! You could see the gaps if you listened hard, there was that bit where stupid Orsino left out half a speech, but everyone carried on. And Malvolio nearly bumped into Maria etc though they were supposed to be hiding out of sight. And when Orsino said, 'If music be the food of love, play on,' nobody did, on Thursday.

But it was really really good. I was out front and I clapped and clapped – felt really jealous of Viola when he came on holding her hand at the end. How clever he is to make something as good as that out of us lot. I feel further away from him than ever.

**Sunday 11th November**
Feel so tired and depressed. Mum keeps saying, 'Do

stop mooching about, Hannah.' And Ruthie's in one of her irritating manic moods. But all I want to do is sit and watch rubbish movies on telly. And eat! Oh my God, Mum had made apple tart for their dinner party last night and there was some left over. I made such a *pig* of myself. Rice cakes for you, now, all week, Hannah.

Of course I know all about bulimia, and yes, it's a bad thing. But surely, if you really controlled being sick – and didn't throw up more than once a day or so, it couldn't hurt, could it?

Don't worry, dear diary, I'm not going to try it!

**Monday 12th November**

I think . . . I'm a bit scared, actually. But I'm happy today. I think I am.

I managed to catch up with him after school, in the road. No reason why I shouldn't talk to my English teacher. Anyway, I really did have something to ask him. I explained about Grace's wedding poems, and how they couldn't be Shakespeare and so on and how I had no ideas at all. He laughed, and said, 'Leave it with me, Hannah. I'll think about it.'

Then we got to where he turns off for the Underground and I turn off for the bus. And then suddenly he's calling out after me. I go back and we face each other. 'Listen, Hannah,' he says, and spreads out his hands with a laugh. 'I don't know if I'm being . . . Well, tell me to shut up if you want . . . but I just wondered if you might like to come and help me pick them out yourself . . . '

I stare at him. What is he trying to say?

'It's just that . . . well, Jenny and the kids will be away this weekend on some Outward Bound course in Cumbria . . . Of course it wouldn't matter if they were around . . . But, well I have to stay in, because there's someone's coming to mend the washing machine at some unspecified time – you know how these people are . . . '

Now I know what he's saying. He's asking me to his house when his wife and family are going to be away.

I feel quite faint and distant, as if I'm being swept away. I don't feel like a real person, standing there in the street, clutching a Next carrier bag. I feel like a sea-nymph or a mermaid, all swimmy and glittering and shimmery, about to fade from view any moment. I'm not a real person so it doesn't matter what I say.

I say Yes.

# Chapter Six

**Friday 16th November**

All week I've just been sleep-walking. Luckily, Mum's so busy she hasn't noticed anything amiss, and Dad wouldn't notice anything anyway.

But something is telling me that nothing will ever be the same after Saturday, and I'm scared. And another bit of me says, what a coward, to be frightened of love, and remember you do believe in the holiness of the heart's affections.

And another part of me says, you're only going to pick out some poems, for Christ's sake. Why all the drama?

**Sunday 18th November**

Well, I must write it down, all of it, and hope that that way it will all make sense. I feel...

I don't know what I feel. Writing it down will help.

So I dress myself (carefully casual – nice jeans, grey t-shirt and fleece – no make-up) and set off, having presented Mum with the usual carefully prepared not-quite-true story (going to do some revision at a friend's house). I leave myself heaps of time though it's only three stops on the Tube, with the result that I'm horribly early, so I walk round and round. It's quite dreary out here – I've never been here before – just rows and rows of little houses all the same. I walk past his house three times; it's red brick and semi-detached with a rather untidy front garden. The door is painted quite a nice blue, and there's a faded Neighbourhood Watch sticker and a poster in the window about some Sports Day. It's so much smaller than our house – and I feel a twinge of guilt. What must he have thought when he took me home? Our house must have seemed so grand to him and yet, he's cleverer and better than all of us put together…

Eventually I pluck up courage and ring the doorbell. I'm very conscious of the smell of some bitter winter shrub and newish paint. The door opens, and he's standing there, in jeans, which I've never seen him wear, and a big old sweater. He ushers me inside, and when the door is closed behind us, kisses me lightly on the cheek. 'Thank you for coming, Hannah,' he says.

His house has that different smell that all other people's houses have. I try to take it in, because this is what surrounds him every day, and I want to share it. We go into the living room, which has slightly shabby polished boards, a few bright rugs, a couple of blue sofas, and piles of books. It's nice. There's a pair of running shoes hurled into a corner and a hockey stick. Books and magazines are piled around, slightly chaotic, but not out of control.

He stands in the middle of the room, and smiles at me. 'Hannah,' he says.

He offers coffee and though I feel sick to my stomach, I say yes, because it's something to do. While he's gone, I look at the bookshelves. There's a sprawl of novels, history, poetry. And a shelf of fitness books which must belong to his wife. There aren't any photos of his wife and children, though.

He comes back with the coffee. I don't hear him coming in and it makes me jump a little. He says, 'Would you believe it, after all that the electrician phoned to cancel. Anyway, we can relax a little. Milk? Sugar?'

Like an idiot, I say Yes to sugar. He must think me such a slob.

We make polite conversation. Did I have trouble getting here? Finding the house? The Tube's so bad these days, but the bus takes forever. He ought to cycle in really. And so on.

Then he says, 'Well, so what about these poems?' He sits down and pats the sofa next to him. 'I had a quick skim through the shelves before you came,' he said, and I'm touched to see that there's a pile of books there.

'Weddings,' I say with what's meant to be a sophisticated little laugh, only it comes out as a sort of high-pitched squawk. 'They're such a hassle.'

'They certainly are,' he agrees. 'I remember Jen's mother refusing to talk to me because she thought I wasn't good enough for her daughter.'

I don't know what to say to this. It reminds me of things I don't want to think about. Anyway, I go and sit next to him. The sofa sags. He's gone all serious. 'Now, Hannah, I did have a quick look but it's surprisingly difficult to find love poems that are happy and suitable to be read out in church. There's a nice one here by Philip Sidney. And here's an American one, by Emily Dickinson, which might be suitable. And – oh, it's very well-known of course, but I thought this one might work. It's by Elizabeth Barratt Browning. You probably know it.'

'I'm not sure.'

'Well, shall I read it to you and you can tell me?'

'Okay.'

His voice is very matter of fact and teacherly. But he starts reading. In his ordinary voice at first.

*How do I love thee? Let me count the ways…*

But you can't read a poem like this in an ordinary voice. Soon, it's as though everything in the world has stopped moving and is listening to his voice. I can feel the beat of my heart, the blood rushing through my ears like a raging torrent. I look at him, at the stern profile of his face and I think how for so long I've looked at him across a classroom, and now here I am sitting on his sofa and he's reading a love poem. To me…

Oh Hannah, Hannah, I want to say, stop it, don't be such a moron. Can't you see what's happening?

But I know she isn't going to stop. Not now...

I do sort of know the poem. At least I thought I did. But I've never really listened to it.

*I love thee with the passion put to use*
*In my old griefs, and with my childhood's faith.*
*I love thee with a love I seemed to lose*
*With my lost saints...*

And then he's finished. Slowly he closes the book and rests it on his lap. I'm looking at him, but he doesn't look at me. There's a long long silence. I don't think even the clock is ticking. I think my heart is going to swell up and stop beating altogether.

Then he says, 'Oh, Hannah.'

He's still not looking at me.

I say, 'Why didn't you talk to me?'

Now he looks at me, puzzled.

'At school this week. You've been so unfriendly.'

He sighs, a deep, long sigh. 'Oh Hannah, Hannah. I thought you could guess the reason for that.'

'I thought you didn't like me any more.'

'If you only knew.'

Another long long silence.

Then he says, 'It's not right, Hannah. You know that.'

'What isn't right?'

And at last he looks at me. His face looks haggard. 'The... feelings I have for you, Hannah.'

And it dawns on me at last what he's saying.

'Perhaps I have those feelings too,' I say in a little voice.

'That doesn't make them right.'

'The holiness of the heart's affections. You told us that yourself.'

He smiles, a little. 'Now you're using my words against me.'

'Keats' words.'

'Keats. I wonder what he really knew about it, anyway.'

'He was a poet. Poets know.'

'Poets know nothing, Hannah. I've come to believe that. Love isn't a blessing. Quite the opposite.'

I find my voice.

'I love you,' I say. I've never said it before to anyone.

He laughs again. 'And I love you, too, Hannah. But what does it mean?'

'It just means I love you. I can't say any more than that.'

'But I'm old enough to be your father, for Christ's sake.'

'That doesn't matter. Why should that matter?'

'Plus I'm your bloody teacher.'

'No one need find out.'

He buries his head in his hands.'If only I had your clear view of things . . . Oh Hannah, Hannah, what a mess.'

I don't mean to but I find I'm crying. He must think I'm a real wuss.

He jumps to his feet and gets me a tissue from a box. 'Hannah, don't do that. You're breaking my heart.'

And suddenly, just as I'd always imagined, we're in each other's arms.

And he's kissing me, and I'm kissing him.

I could have stayed like that for ever, just kissing. But it doesn't stay like that. I can hear him breathing hard and then he's inside my clothes, all over me.

I'll do anything to make him happy, anything.

Nat and I never went all the way. We used to joke about it. He'd call me The Last Notting Hill Virgin, and say, don't worry, Hannah, I'll wear you down in the end, just you see. He was good about it, I guess, for a boy. But somehow, I never wanted to, with him.

I'm scared, so scared. But I know he won't hurt me. And this is what love is all about, isn't it? What right have I to back off?

And I think it's too late, now.

He breathes in my ear, 'Is this what you want, Hannah? Say it's what you want me to do.'

What if I said no, now? Yes, I say, it's what I want.

He's got a condom from somewhere. Part of me registers that I'm glad, another part just wonders how he's found it so conveniently. I guess men always carry them, don't they?

And then I gasp out. It hurts, at first. I clutch him to me.

Then it's all over. We're slumped in a heap on the sofa. He's still breathing heavily for a long while. Then he says, 'That was your first time, wasn't it, Hannah?'

'Yes,' I confess.

'I'm sorry,' he says.

'Don't be.'

'I love you, my little Hannah,' he says.

It's done. There's no going back now.

# Chapter Seven

It's so weird, standing in his kitchen, in this new changed world while he makes more coffee. He offers me a sandwich but I don't want one – I couldn't bear him to watch me eating. Sometimes he smiles at me. *This is my lover*, I think, but I can't get my head around it. We talk about a lot of things. I tell him how clever everyone in my family is, and how I feel like the outsider. Which perhaps isn't the sort of thing I should be saying to him, but it all just comes out. He tells me that his marriage is basically dead. He says they only stick together because of the children, and as soon as they're old enough, he's sure they'll split. He says he loved me almost as soon as he saw me – he said I wasn't like the usual girls of my age and there was something timeless about me. I don't know what he means but I like the sound of it. And he wonders how I can fancy an old man like he is. I say that isn't a problem – it's always happening in Hollywood. After all, I'm not underage. There's nothing wrong, though I agree with him, we'll have to keep things discreet at school...

I want him to make love to me again. This time I want to understand what it's all about. But he doesn't try to touch me again. He seems a bit nervous, and I can understand that. After all, it's his own house. I say, should I go, and he says, maybe it would be for the best. He says he'll photocopy the poems and bring them in – I like the way he doesn't forget things like that.

I think I'd better go now – it'll be easier for him. He says, 'You're wonderful, Hannah. I don't deserve you.'

We kiss again, in the dark hallway. And then I'm outside, blinking in the cold winter sunlight.

But I told them at home I'd be out all day. I don't want to go home yet. So when I get the train, I stay on it, all the way to Marble Arch. I can even plan my Christmas shopping, I guess.

I walk through the crowds. I go into Selfridges and try on lipstick and drench myself with perfume. I wander through Marks, holding horrible tops up against myself as though I want to see what they look like. I trail silk scarves against my hand, cerise, burnt orange, holly green, enjoying the soft feel of the fabric. I remember his hands on my body and his mouth against mine. I wander round and round. I bet every store detective has their eyes on me, Hannah, the mad girl. I go into a bookshop. There's a new bestseller, a love story. I could write my own now, I think. I go to the poetry shelves to see if I can find Elizabeth Barratt Browning, but she's not there. I even go into a sandwich shop and buy a big sugary doughnut, but luckily I catch myself before I've sunk my teeth into it, and I throw it away, into a bin, in disgust.

I walk on, but something makes me turn round. There's somebody at the bin. Disgusting. They saw me throw the doughnut away and they're scavenging. It's a girl with long dark hair. She's wearing jeans and a dark fleece. Her hair falls over her face, and then she raises it, as she picks the sticky paper bag out from the horrible mess in the bin. She lifts it up triumphantly and waves it in the air.

As she does, she looks me straight in the eyes, and smiles at me. The studs in her lip and the bruises have gone. Her face is hard and pale. Her eyes are cold. I know her face well. I see it in the mirror every day of my life.

And now I know what I haven't known before.

She hates me. She wants me dead.

When I've finished reading this, I feel as though I've been punched in the gut. It's like standing there in the street watching while an old lady is beaten up or someone's cruel to an animal. I want to take her and shake her by the shoulders and say, For God's sake, Hannah, you stupid cow, wise up! You've let yourself get shagged by a dirty old man and you talk about it as though it's something magic! It's the oldest trick in the book, Hannah, you idiot, and you've fallen for it!

And I want to punch her beloved Mr Sinclair hard in the face.

But there's something else that's troubling me about what I've been reading. As though I've been ignoring something that should have been staring me in the face.

I don't know what it is. It's there, but I can't see it, only sense its troubling shadow.

I can't read any more today. Anyway, I'm off to see Cara.

'Cara,' I say over our usual pizza, 'could you fancy a teacher?'

She throws back her head and gives me her raucous laugh.

'A teacher? There's that new guy in the games department. He's really cool.'

Fair enough. I know who she means. He's about twenty-three, with a fuzz of dark hair and great muscles. I bet he works out. I could almost fancy him myself. But that's not what I meant.

'No, I mean a *real* teacher. An old one.'

'What, like old Woolcott? Or Frogface?'

'Yes, or Pittsie . . .'

'Pittsie's a really good teacher. But *fancy* him. You must be joking.'

'Yeah, that's what I thought.'

'You're asking some dead peculiar questions these days.'

'Sorry.'

'Is anything wrong?'

'No. Why do you ask?'

'I don't know. You've just been different lately. Like you've got something on your mind.'

'Well, I haven't. Not really.'

And then an image jumps into my mind, just for a fraction of a second. I see a wide flat beach, and the glitter of the sea at the end of the day. There are dunes and our garden stretches right down to them. I remember the evening well. It was last year, when Cara and her mum asked me down to spend a week with them at the cottage they were renting by the sea in Norfolk. It was a great evening. We took our food out into the garden, and ate watching the sea and the sunset. Seagulls wheeled in the air, and I can still smell the salty wind as I think about it now in the fug of the pizza parlour.

I remember the evening all right. But what I don't remember is why I remembered it and why it seems suddenly vital to find out.

Anyway, it's gone now. And I'm dying to get back to Hannah's story and find out what happened after Mr Perv had his wicked way with her.

**Monday 19th November**

Being in love is working wonders for the diet – I just don't feel hungry this morning so skipping breakfast is no problem.

It's been such a strange weekend. And luckily everyone's been too busy to take much notice of me. Mum is going to be on TV! 'The Money Programme' is doing a piece on successful small companies like hers and they're going to come and make this documentary of us at home. I suppose they're going to make her a sort of housewife-superstar. They're coming to do it on Friday, and Mum wants us all there. Even Grace has to put in an appearance and Felix is being enticed down for the weekend. I keep telling her that I won't be able to make it on Friday, though. We're joining up with six other schools to do this Conference on the Future of the World – Is This The End Of Western Civilisation? It's a bit of a stupid idea, but Miss Ridgeway has organised it and is getting all excited about it. Anyway, I'm supposed to be a good speaker so I'm going to take part. It was all arranged weeks ago, only I kind of forgot about it. So I won't be home that evening until late. I keep trying to tell Mum, but she isn't listening. I expect you'll be able to get away, is all she says. She's so wrapped up in it, and what it might mean for her business that she can't hear anything else. Anyway, I don't suppose me being there or not there will really make any difference to anything.

Today at school is strange. We have Double English after break, and he and I don't really register each other. He's giving us background notes about *The Tempest*, so there's a lot of him talking and us writing things down. Sometimes it seems just like a normal lesson and then I look at him and remember what happened. I can't put it all together yet.

But I shan't hassle him. This must be really hard for him. I'm going to show him that I can be sensible and understanding.

But I wish he'd talk to me again.

**Tuesday 20th November.**

As usual I gave half my sandwiches to Candy. I've managed to persuade Mum to leave out the mayonnaise and use only low-fat spread. I've convinced her it's much better and she seems to have got the message. The evening meal is a problem, though! I have to tread very carefully if I don't want to stuff myself full of calories. I don't want to upset Mum; she's so proud of her cooking. The thing to do is to help yourself rather than having someone help you. Then you can spread it about the plate so it looks more than it is, and if you keep moving your knife and fork nobody notices you're not eating so much. It sounds mean, but it's the only way!

**Wednesday 21st November**

I met him walking across the playground to the Junior Block. I caught up with him and we walked together. There's nothing unusual in that – no one would have noticed a girl talking to her teacher.

I didn't know what to say, though. He spoke first. He said, 'Hannah, my feelings haven't changed one bit. But you know it's going to be difficult.'

'I know. I'll be really patient. But when are we going to be together again?'

'I can't say, just now. But leave it with me. I'll think of something. I have to go now.'

I'll be patient. I'll wait as long as he wants. I'll do whatever it takes.

# Chapter Eight

**Thursday 22nd November**

I've been thinking, and I've made some plans. Our relationship is only 'wrong' as long as I'm at school. But I don't have to stay at school forever. I can't leave straightaway as I expect Mum and Dad have to give some sort of notice with the fees, but I could leave at the end of the summer term. Only two and a half terms away! I could get myself a job of some sort – I'm sure I could be an office junior somewhere and maybe work in a bar in the evenings if I needed a tad more, just till I found my feet. Then there would be nothing to stop us seeing each other! I wouldn't expect him even to leave his wife, not yet. I can see that it might be hard just to walk out. But he's told me that the marriage is dead and they just inhabit the same space. (I can't imagine that they still have sex together, though he didn't mention that. I'd like to ask him about that but I don't quite know how.) So the present situation can't be any more fun for her than it is for him. She might even be quite glad of an excuse to get away herself.

When I'm working, I should be able to find myself a room somewhere – though I don't suppose I'll be able to afford anything as nice as my present room, not for years! And then – then – he can come and visit. Maybe eventually even move in. Being married or not isn't important to me – I must make sure he knows that. I don't mind if I never get married. After all it's just a show. If someone really loves you and you really love someone you don't need a bit of paper to give you permission.

But I don't want him to feel that he's under any pressure to leave his wife. That would be really stupid of me – I wouldn't want to panic him. All I want – at first, anyway – is to have him when he can manage it. Maybe later on, I might want things to be more permanent, I don't know. But for a while just having him there would be enough for me, and knowing that he loves me.

And I know he does. He told me, in his kitchen, that he couldn't ever remember feeling this way about anyone else before. He said at first he tried to struggle against it, when he realised what was happening to him. But then he knew that the struggle wasn't working. He says that in all his years, he's never known anything like this. He thought he was in love before, once or twice, but compared to what he feels for me, it was nothing.

He called me the love of his life.

So I will do everything for him.

Of course, it will cause problems here at home – I can't help that. The idea here is that I'll go to university like Grace and Felix. Nobody asks you if you want to go – it's just taken for granted. And normally, I'd have been happy to go. Was almost looking forward to it. But all that's changed, now. I shall have to choose my time carefully, and then tell them. Maybe sometime after Christmas. Of course I won't mention *him*. There's no point and *nobody* must know about us, or he'd lose his job. He loves teaching and he's such a brilliant teacher. I couldn't do that to him.

Mum and Dad will both be upset. At least Mum will – I don't know so much about Dad. Remember that time when I was eight and I won that poetry prize at school! It was a really dumb poem about world peace and everyone loving each other, but never mind. I bounced home so excitedly. When Dad came home I was all over him – *Daddy, Daddy, guess what, I won the prize for my poem!*

And all he said was, 'Now, where did I put that file? Did you, darling, that's nice.'

And he left the room. Of course I cried and cried. Even Grace and Felix tried to be nice. They said, 'Well done, kid.' But it wasn't the same as Dad.

Mum said, 'I know it must feel a little disappointing for you, but you must remember, darling, that we're all very privileged to have someone like Daddy in our family. And it's not that he doesn't care, he really does. But he has such important things on his mind.'

So I suppose whatever I do it'll never be quite enough to make him really pleased. Someone like him just doesn't have time to notice what other people are doing or thinking. Mum notices, of course, and I know she was really pleased when Felix got his scholarship and when

Grace got her First. But that also means that there's nothing left for me to do that hasn't already been done by someone else. And the good side of that is, that it means it won't hurt them as much as it would if I was, say, an only child.

And I can't see any harm in starting off with some crap job in an office. You don't need qualifications these days – loads of people start off making the tea and end up running the company. So I might even benefit from it!

It's going to be all right; it's going to be all right. The holiness of the heart's affections – it's got to be right!

It's this debate thing tomorrow – I'd much rather not do it and I'm feeling a bit nervous. But it'll soon be over.

Oh, Hannah, Hannah, you are being such a dork. And that precious family of yours aren't helping much, if you don't mind me saying.

I keep thinking, if only someone would just sit down with you and give you a good talking-to, it might make you see sense.

And then again, it probably wouldn't. If even your friend Nat, who sounds a bit too good to be true, if you ask me, can't get through to you, then I don't know who can.

Your *ex*-friend Nat, I should say, because you've dumped him, haven't you?

The trouble is, I'm finding that I can't stop thinking about you. Even Cara thinks I've got something on my mind. But I keep going over and over it. I switch between wanting to give you a bollocking to bring you to your senses, and giving you a big hug and letting you cry on my shoulder. Sometimes I think you're being so dumb, you deserve everything that's happening to you, and then I think – no, nobody deserves this.

I wonder what's happened now. Is it all over? I don't even know *when* you wrote your bloody diary...

...Yes, I do now. That gave me an idea. I went and found my last year's diary, and the days and dates match. It's March now, just about, so all of this was just happening at the end of last year. So one way or another, something must have been resolved.

But which way?

And why do I keep thinking of the night in Norfolk by the sea? What did happen that night?

Got to go. Mum's calling.

Mum and Cara were sitting in the living room when I went down. They were having a good girly gossip. Mum should have had a daughter, I guess. Sometimes I feel I'm surplus to requirements there. Actually, Cara likes Mum because she's more down to earth than her mum, who's barking. Cara's mum works in a Women's Health Co-operative just off Portobello; she's into crystals and aromatherapy and whale music and foot massage. If it's dead or mad, she believes in it. Cara is all for reason and common sense, and her mum drives her crazy. Though she's quite fun and very entertaining on a good day.

It occurred to me when I went in that it would actually be a good opportunity to tell them both about Hannah's diary. After all, it's only a few days since I found it, though it feels like forever. I start putting together the way I want to introduce the subject. 'Listen, while you're both together, I need your advice . . .' 'Listen, there's something I ought to tell you . . .' (No, that sounds as though I've done something wrong, and I haven't.) 'Listen, I want to show you something . . .'

But they're absorbed in their own conversation. Mum's reading the local paper (the most scary thing since *The Texas Chainsaw Massacre*, if you ask me) and they're locked in female indignation over something. 'I can't imagine that nobody's missed her!' 'It's really dreadful when you think about it.' 'What are we coming to, I wonder, when something like this can happen . . .' etc, etc. They're talking about the body they found in the park a few months ago. There was police tape everywhere and we couldn't get to school. She was probably a druggy, but no one seemed to know. After a few days everyone forgot about it. The local paper can't seem to find anything new to say, other than the mystery still hasn't been solved and no one knows who she is. I can think of all sorts of reasons why people might want to get away from their families (not mine, Mum, honest!) but to Cara and Mum that's heresy. They go on for a bit more, saying how shocking, and what a world we live in. The upshot is, that by the time they've finished and we're getting round to interesting matters like, When will the Spag Bog be ready and can I have masses of grated cheese?, I've lost the urge to talk about Hannah and her diary.

I'll sort it out someday.

# Chapter Nine

**Friday 23rd November**

Oh, I don't know. Sometimes I wonder if I have a mind at all, I keep changing it so often. I felt so grown-up and in control yesterday, making all those plans and today it feels so different.

Today he just didn't even *look* at me. He seemed to be avoiding my gaze and instead at the end of the lesson went off with Millie and Katya – *flirting* with them.

No, of course he wasn't flirting. But that's what it looked like.

And when I passed him going the other way a bit later (I'd been lying in wait for him outside the library because I knew he was on his way to the Lower Fourth) he didn't even raise his eyes, just walked past.

And I can't bear it! I want him here, now! It's so unfair, Tasha is going on and on about her bloody Ben. They're back together now, at least for the moment they are, and it's all lovey-dovey. 'I just can't wait for tomorrow! Ooh I can't wait! Mum and Dad are going out! Tee-hee! While the cat's away. Ooh I can't wait!' And so on.

Why can't it be like that for me? Why can't I have a boyfriend I can talk about, can admit to?

Look at the smug stuff I wrote yesterday. Don't want

to panic him, don't want to put pressure on him! How did I write all that? I just want to scream out at him in the middle of class, I just want to rush up to him and hold him. I want him here, now. I want to know what's going to happen to us. I can't possibly wait even until next summer. I can't wait a week. I can't wait a day. I can't wait five minutes.

His wife is a bitch cow dog. I hate her, I hate her. I wish she had cancer. I hope she gets run over tomorrow by a large lorry.

And sometimes I love him so much I hate him too. Oh, what am I going to do?

**Saturday 24th November.**

No breakfast again, and just an apple for lunch. I've lost two pounds!!!!!!

Well, at least there's something I'm doing right. I mustn't let myself down. I mustn't become that fat disgusting self I was two months ago. Not now. I held up that pink skirt that I used to bulge out of. Rolls of fat. How could I bear to be seen out like that?

I must NEVER NEVER get that way again.

I must be nearly down to size ten now. What if I could be size eight by the wedding? Then nobody could say that Daniel's sisters looked like little birds next to me.

**Monday 26th November**

Another weird day. Oh I don't know. But something good happened at last.

Miss R wanted someone to show her something on the computer, at which, like all adults, she's a complete dork. So I phoned home and left a message to say I'd be late, which was just as well.

Anyway, I sorted out her problem which wasn't really very challenging, in about twenty minutes, and set off home. Nearly everyone had gone by then and the cleaners were coming in. Outside it was dark and drizzly – a real midwinter day. I left the school gates, went down the road and across the green, and was just turning the corner, when a car drew up beside me. I thought it might be some perv so I didn't turn round, and began to walk faster. I could hear the car creeping up the road beside me, and just as I was about to run, a door opened, and a voice said, 'Gone off me already, have you?' I turned, and it was him! 'Hop in, you idiot, quick, before anyone sees!'

I looked around, but the streets were deserted. No one saw me. I jumped in the car, quick as quick, slammed the door, and we drove off, laughing like conspirators.

'Have you got five minutes?' he said.

'Oh yes. I already told them I was going to be late.'

'I know a quietish street in Chiswick. We can park the car there and have a bit of a talk. Suit you?'

Oh yes, oh yes, it suited me. We dived into the rush hour main road traffic for a bit, but soon lost it as he zapped into back roads. We ended up – I don't know where, but it was a quiet car park, by an empty office block, quite near the river.

He stopped the car, breathed out deeply, and then turned to me. 'Well,' he said, with a smile. 'So how've you been?'

Idiot, I'd meant to be calm and cool, but it all came out in a rush as though I was a sulky five-year-old. 'Why wouldn't you even look at me the other day?'

'Be sensible, Hannah. Why do you think?'

'Because you don't like me any more?'

'Come here and I'll show you just how much I don't like you any more.'

So I did. If every moment could be like this, then nothing else would matter.

'I can't let people see that's how I think of you,' he whispered into my ear, between kissing me till I thought I would explode with joy.

So I didn't say any more about him flirting with Katya and Millie, and the horrible thoughts I'd had about his wife.

'How's your week been?' he said.

'So peculiar. I've been like a zombie. Luckily, I don't think anyone's noticed. But just trying to be a normal person, it feels so weird.'

'I know. Everyone rushing around, fussing over lost kit and missing keys and files in the wrong place and the phone going and the cat hissing and the telly blaring and the doors slamming. And you just want to say, stop, everyone, stop. I want to go away and think my nice Hannah-thoughts.'

'And do you?'

'All the time,' he said, kissing me again.

I feel all right again. All the bits of the me-jigsaw are in place instead of being jumbled up in a plastic bag. This is all I need, I think. So simple.

At least it would have been if idiot Hannah had managed to keep her mouth shut. Instead she goes blathering on.

'You haven't managed to tell your wife yet?'

'Hannah!'

'You said you would.'

'I know. And I will.'

'When, though?'

'Hannah, you aren't thinking this through. If I tell Jen now, then all hell will break loose. My world will literally come crashing down. There'll be lawyers, recriminations. There'll be a divorce, in which *you* would be cited. I'd lose my house – have to move into a flat. I'd also lose my job and my source of income. Now I wouldn't be much good to you in those circumstances.'

'I guess not. I just want you, that's all.'

'Do you think I don't want you? Well then, shut up.'

And he kissed me again. 'Little thin shoulders,' he said into my neck. 'Are you sure you're eating enough, Hannah?'

'I'm an absolute pig. Listen. I've been thinking too.' And I told him my idea, about leaving school in the summer and getting a job and a room. I thought he'd be pleased but he didn't say anything for ages. 'You can't do that,' he said finally. 'You can't give up school. What about university?'

'Everyone says university as though it's the answer to life. I don't want to go to university.'

'But you can't throw your life away.'

'I wouldn't be. I'd be being with you.'

'Yes, but... Oh, I don't know. We'll have to talk this through. Promise me you won't do anything hasty.'

'I promise. But I've made my mind up.'

'Look,' he said. 'You're young, everything's ahead of you. I'd never forgive myself if you gave everything up now, just because of me. I'll do my best to think of some solution to all this. But in the meantime, just hold tight, will you? Promise?'

'I promise.'

'Good girl. Now I guess we'd better get you home.'

When I arrive home, my head's spinning so that I can hardly think straight. I'd intended to rush upstairs and hide myself in my room. But somebody calls out to me and I go into the living room. There I'm met by an unusual sight. The whole family, nearly – Mum, Ruthie, Grace and even Dad – *watching television!* Mum never watches television. But there they all are sitting glued to the box.

'Look at this,' calls Mum, 'they've sent a video of the rushes they did that day the television crew were here. They're going to edit this, of course, but Nigel thought we'd like to have the shots of the family to keep.'

I come into the living room, to see our kitchen immortalised on screen. Mum is chopping away at some vegetables, while holding forth to the camera about some facet of economic policy.

'You should have seen your face when the camera picked you up,' giggled Ruthie. 'Like, hey, what is going on?'

'I thought you looked really good,' said Grace.

'But I can't have done. I wasn't there.'

'Of course you were *there*, stupid. We just saw you.'

'But I wasn't. I was at school. It was the evening of the debate-thing. I told you.'

'You were still here.'

'Hannah, stop being so obstreperous. Ruth, wind the tape back a bit, will you?'

Ruth rewound it a bit, and then started playing it. I saw myself coming into the room, looking startled as the camera picked me up, then smiling and blowing it a kiss. I picked up some books from the table and wandered out again. The door shut behind me.

Only it wasn't me. I wasn't there that night. I was in our school hall defending Western civilisation to a hundred other kids and thirty teachers from assorted London schools.

I don't know what's going on. I'm really frightened.

# Chapter Ten

And it's at this moment, as I just read those words, that what I've been trying to remember comes back to me. It comes back all in a rush, like when that ketchup bottle you've been vainly shaking for hours suddenly disgorges a lake of red goo all over your chips.

Now I remember that evening even more clearly, and I remember the day which led up to it. It had been a really good day. Cara's mum had rented this little cottage, all white walls and curtains blowing in the salty wind and bright bright sea light. I'd been down for a couple of days – I think I spent two more days, but it rained for both of those.

Cara's mum had spent the day exploring some of the local fish markets. Cara and I had been doing some exploring of our own, so we were happy and giggly and very pleased with ourselves.

The sun was just going down and Cara's mum had laid the table within sight of the sea. It was only a plastic picnic table, but she'd covered it with a piece of African cloth. There were some yellow daisies in a jar and some nightlights burning away in little glass jars all over the place. It looked really great – Cara's mum can do things like that, turn just an ordinary evening meal into a party.

She'd put the fresh seafood she'd bought into a pasta number, and though it had taken ages to get going, it was worth waiting for. Now we were sitting there, completely stuffed, looking at the last shreds of sunlight on the dark glittering sea. I had sand in my shoes and in my belly button and ears. I'd be burned from the sun the next day, but today I just felt pleasantly tingly.

Somehow, we'd got onto the subject of ghosts and hauntings. It wasn't a surprising subject, given Cara's mum, but the surprising thing was that Cara was going along with it. It shows how relaxed and happy Cara must have been feeling.

I remember Cara's mum's face in the evening light, lit up by the flickering candles. It was Cara's nice, ugly expressive face a few years on, with the difference that Cara would never have worn those daft dangly earrings or that mixture of colours and stripes. She was talking about this town, which had once existed further down the coast, a real town with churches and shops and streets and big houses. Over the years it had gradually crumbled away into the sea, so that nothing was there now except a small village, and even that was getting smaller every year as the sea attacked the coast. She had us both fascinated as she told us of the legends about this place, the drowned steeples, the ghostly bells, the glowing lights, the mysterious sightings that fishermen and walkers along the shore had told of. Even the normally scathing Cara was rapt.

I suppose that had softened us up, for then we went on

to have a full-blown conversation about ghosts and hauntings. Cara's mum held us spellbound as she told us of abbeys where nuns who'd had lovers had been walled up alive, or great houses where servant girls had been seduced by evil masters and killed themselves before giving birth. There were houses deep in the country where girls who would not marry their father's choice of horrible old men had been locked in their bedrooms for the rest of their lives, scratching their sad little names on the window glass with diamond rings. Cara's mum said that all these people could leave their sadness imprinted on a place, so that the air was charged with it ever after. Then there were victims of terrible crimes whose spirits were unable to rest until justice had been done to them. Then there were the evil-doers themselves, people so bad that even Satan didn't want them in Hell, so they stalked the earth, full of malice. Sometimes, the ghost of a happy child might inhabit a garden and leave everyone who went there feeling strangely happy too. There were good ghosts and bad ghosts, Cara's mother said, happy ghosts and sad ghosts, restless ghosts and contented ghosts, ghosts full of evil, and ghosts who brought only good. It was great stuff, and sitting there, by the shimmering night sea, you had to half believe it, even if your daytime self would have scoffed.

And then she said, 'You know, some people have even seen their own ghost. It's supposed to have happened to several people in Holland Park, for example. It's called a Fetch, your own ghost.'

Cara chortled. 'Holland Park? Well, there are plenty of weirdos there. But I've never seen my own ghost.'

'And you don't want to, my girl. Because if you do, it's a sign you're going to die.'

Cara and I were supposed to be meeting up with the gang that evening. We started off in the pub on the corner (two Coca-Colas, naturally. Underage drinking? *Moi?*). I'd been in a funny mood, and like anyone else in a funny mood, the last thing I was going to do was admit it. Being in that frame of mind makes me tease and niggle. I know, I can feel myself doing it, but it's better than having one of those heart-to-hearts that girls love.

In the end, we never get to where the gang are hanging out. We're just sipping our Cokes slowly and going round in conversational circles. Cara's saying, 'Look, do you want this or not? I don't want to be out with you if you're going to be in a strop all evening.'

I said, 'I'm not in a strop. Don't bug me, woman.'

'See? I can't have a sensible conversation with you.'

I put on my Mafia-Godfather voice, 'Listen, you wanna sensible conversation, we have a sensible conversation, okay?'

'Tom, just shut up, will you?'

'You wanna shut me up, you gotta make me an offer I can't refuse.'

'Tom!'

'Okay,' I say in my normal voice. 'Sorry.'

'Tom, just what is bugging you, right?'

'I keep telling you, nothing's bugging me.'

'You've been dead peculiar lately. There is something. Have you met another girl or something?'

'No, of course not.'

'Then, *what*?'

'Nothing. Nothing's changed.'

'Listen,' said Cara. 'We're really good together. I really like you. But I'm telling you one thing, Tom, I can't stand people who lie to me. If you're lying to me, then I promise you, it's over.'

**Wednesday 28th November.**

This morning, when we were all straggling out of our English lesson, he catches up with me in the corridor. Without breaking his stride or changing his expression, he says in a voice so low that only I can hear it, 'Listen, you're working late in the library tonight, right?' I don't look up at him, but just say, 'Yes,' back, in as neutral a tone as I can manage.

The rest of the day passes in a haze. After school, I pile up my things and go into the old building where the library is. There's another girl working there. I spread my things over a table that gives me a good viewpoint of all the doors and try to concentrate. After a while the other girl gets up and goes. She says, 'Cheers,' to me, with a smile. I smile back, weakly. The minutes tick by. Ten, fifteen.

Miss Ridgeway comes in. She says, 'Hannah, you work too hard, you know. You know what they say about all work and no play!' Then she takes a huge volume from the shelf and plonks herself down on a chair, and starts to read.

Another five minutes. I've gone rigid with nerves. I've been reading the same line over and over, and stringing numbers and dates down the page as if I'm going to write notes.

The library is silent as a tomb. The plaster busts over the door stare down at me reproachfully. Shakespeare, Plato, Newton. They all disapprove. There's a huge Victorian painting over the fireplace, a string of maidens all dressed in white holding garlands of flowers. We used to speculate what they were getting so worked up about. We call them the Sacrificial Virgins. I think of all the girls, over the years who've sat in this room working away and I wonder if any of them have ever had the thoughts I'm having now.

Miss Ridgeway breathes a huge sigh and shuts the book with a snap. Clouds of dust puff out. She has bad legs and lives with her mother in Tufnell Park. Once when she was young she went on a cycling holiday around Europe. She often talks of it – I imagine it was the best time of her life.

As she leaves, she smiles down at me. 'Remember, Hannah! All work, no play!' She's so sweet, I feel really mean.

The door shuts behind her. Another five minutes. And finally the little emergency exit at the far end opens just a fraction and I see him there. He looks to see if there's anyone else, then opens it a fraction more. He nods his head to me to indicate that I should follow him up then half closes the door. I leave my things – as if I've just gone for a pee – and go after him.

This is the really old bit of the school, full of winding stairs and doorways and alcoves. I follow him up a narrow uncarpeted stair with ancient fire extinguishers at the bends. One flight, then another. His dark back keeps emerging and disappearing in front of me.

Finally at the top I catch up with him. His face is set. There's a door. He takes out a set of keys, unlocks it and pushes me in, locking it behind us.

It's some kind of old storeroom. There's a little natural light filtering through a tiny window at ceiling level. I can see dusty piles of books all around and on the floor. He takes me in his arms.

Then suddenly we're tumbling in a dusty pile on the floor. His arms are hard and tight. He's whispering my name. I can't get my breath. I hear him gasping. I want to sneeze from the dust. Something is digging into my back.

He's strong, and quick. He's heavy on top of me. It's different this time, no nonsense. I don't have time to rearrange myself and I try not to cry out.

Then it's over, and I hear his long drawn-out breath. I don't know what I'm feeling. He doesn't say anything. Then I don't know why, I start crying. 'What is it now?' he says.

'I don't know. I'm frightened...'

'I'm frightened. We're both frightened.'

'Yes, but . . . '

'But what?'

'I don't think I can handle this . . . '

'Hannah, this is no time for silly schoolgirl stuff. This is grown-up time. You've joined the grown-ups now. Get real, Hannah.'

# Chapter Eleven

**Thursday 29th November**

Go on then, Hannah, you silly bitch. Admit what you did the next day after that. Own up to the Twix bar at lunch and then the crisps. Own up to the double helpings of pasta soaked in cream sauce. Own up to the two slices of filthy rich chocolate goo cake left over from their dinner party. Own up to the disgusting fact that even after that lot, you managed to down not one but *three* biscuits before you went to bed. Own up to the fact that you nearly threw up and just fell on the bed like a great fat lump of lard. You've probably undone all your good intentions of the last few weeks just with that one pigging session.

Hannah, you are a stupid, stupid cow.

**Friday 30th November**

This morning, a group of us were walking across the playground at 9.30. The rest of the school were in Assembly but it was Friday and the Sixth are let off Assembly on Thursday and Friday. With me are Emily, Sarah-Jane, Kezia and Daisy.

A woman's walking briskly across the playground towards us. She's about forty, has curly light brown hair fluffed around her face in one of those not-styles that people with curly hair can get away with, a sensible, pink face with no make-up, and big ginger-brown eyes. She's wearing a dark skirt and flat shoes, with a dark jacket slung over her shoulders. She's vaguely familiar, but I can't place her. She waves to us, and we stop while she catches us up. 'Do you lot know Mr Sinclair?' she says.

Luckily I'm on the end of the line, so she says it to Kezia and Daisy, who are in the middle. She's not looking at my face which is just as well.

'Yes, he's our English teacher,' says Daisy.

'Oh, thank goodness!' she says, with a big, pleasant toothy smile. 'Can you give him something from me? The silly chump went off this morning without his briefcase. He'll be frantic when he finds out.'

'Sure,' says Daisy to whom this is the most casual request in the world. 'We'll see he gets it.'

'Thanks,' she says, 'You're sure to go to Heaven now.'

The others laugh, she laughs too, and then she's off. At the gates she climbs into a black car – the same car that I sat in with *him* the other day – and drives off.

It's her being so smiley that gets me. How dare she smile? How can she smile? The only other time I saw her was at Foundation Evening last year. I think she looked bored. She probably was.

As long as she wasn't real, I didn't have to think about her. But now I know she's there. She's a person.

She's had his babies. She's in my life now, just as she's in his.

Grace is nagging me about the wedding poems. But I can't bear her to have the poem he read to me, at her wedding. She tells me I'm useless. But her friend's got this book which might have something in it. She tells me not to bother. I have to go to be measured for the dress again on Saturday. I'm afraid I'll be just the same size as I was when I first went – ie, a great lump.

I keep thinking I see *her* again. Nearly every day. Only never quite clear enough to be sure. She's there in a crowd surging past, in a bus just zooming out of sight, turning the corner ahead of me and then vanishing.

I think I must be going crazy. Can I keep all this stoppered up inside me and not tell anyone without going mad?

But I'm going to have to.

**Tuesday 4th December**

Oh God. I have just done the most stupid, idiotic, crazy thing I have ever done in my life. I have just opened my mouth and said something so horrible, so mad that I will never be able to put my life together again.

I can hardly bear to write about it.

But I must. It will be my penance.

We'd had a horrible day to begin with. I'd done a really bad Latin translation and Mrs Hale told me off about it. I kept falling asleep in History and even Miss

Ridgeway was in a bad mood. Plus I started getting my period and I felt all clogged up and puffy. My gut ached as though a giant hand was clenching all my insides. I had to borrow a tampax from Daisy, and she uses a different kind from me, and I was sure it was leaking.

I'd meant to throw half my lunch away but Mum had given me a slice of cake and I just ate my way through the lot. Oh God, I can't even manage to be anorexic – I wish I could. I wish I could get so thin I could just fade away.

I really wish that. I'm not just saying it.

It was after that pigged-out lunch that I said what I did. When I walked past the Upper Fourth he was inside, pinning up some essays on a wall display. I opened the door and went in. 'Can I give you a hand?' I said in as normal a voice as I could manage.

'No thanks, Hannah, I'm fine,' he said in a normal voice. And then under his breath, 'You must really be more careful, you know.'

'I know,' I said. 'I just thought after the other day you didn't love me any more.'

He sighed. 'Do you have such a low opinion of me, Hannah?'

'No, but . . .'

'But what?'

'You were so strange.'

'Can't you imagine the strain I'm under?'

'I'm under it too.'

‘It’s different for you. It really is. Now, look, you have to go.’

‘I can’t go on like this. Please.’

‘I told you, Hannah, I’m working on it. I can’t rush this. You must give me time. Now, get back to your friends.’

It was then that I said it. The most stupid thing I have ever said in my whole life. I don’t know why I said it, I didn’t even mean it. I wasn’t going to say it, it just fell out. The second it was out of my mouth I wanted it unsaid. I almost gasped with horror, hearing myself say it.

In one stupid second, you can go and undo so much.

I said, ‘I could tell your wife.’

He didn’t say anything. He just looked at me. I looked back at him. I started to say, ‘No, no, no, I didn’t mean it, I wouldn’t, that was just stupid, please forgive me . . . ’

But he had picked up his things, and had walked out of the room, very fast, without even looking back once.

# Chapter Twelve

**Wednesday 5th December**
He didn't come anywhere near me today.

**Thursday 6th December**
Or today. I can't bear it.

**Friday 7th December**
At last I caught up with him in a corridor. He strode on, eyes fixed ahead.

'What can I say?' I begged him. 'I know it was stupid. I didn't even mean it. I'd never do something like that. I don't know why I said it.'

He said, coldly, 'But you did say it, didn't you? Now go, you're drawing attention to us both.'

**Sunday 9th December**
I went to church with Dad. The priest talked of sin. He said it was fashionable to pretend today that sin didn't exist, that nothing anyone did was bad. He said that was wrong. He said that sin was the poison of the world. He said it ran through our veins like corrosive acid.

He said, there will always be punishment for sin. I'm sure he was looking at me as he spoke.

Nat came round when we were out. Mum sat him in the kitchen and fed him coffee and cakes. She said he was in a bad way about me. She said she couldn't see why I'd dumped him, he is such a nice boy.

I said it was my business.

She said I was being difficult.

I managed lunch pretty well. No roast potatoes. Just some beans. I said I wasn't keen on eating beef. No one seemed to notice – hooray.

Mum has started to plan Christmas. Some of Daniel's family will be here, over for the wedding. She says it will be the best Christmas ever. I can't bear to think about it.

**Wednesday 12th December**

At last we got to talk, and I wish we hadn't. It was lunchtime, and he was in his form room, marking. I said, 'Can I come in?'

He said, 'You've done so already.'

'I'll go, if you want.'

'No. Just don't make any scenes. Don't draw attention to yourself. We need to talk anyway.'

I said, 'I am so so sorry. You know I didn't mean that stupid thing that I said. You know I'd never do anything to hurt you, or to damage what we have.'

He sighed, and scribbled 'C – YOU CAN DO BETTER THAN THIS' on some poor fourth year's essay.

'I wonder just what we do have, Hannah.'

'You know what we have!'

'Yes, I know. I know, for me, anyway. But that business the other day just brought it home to me. Maybe I'm expecting too much of you. Maybe I assumed you were more grown up than you really are.'

That hurt. He looked sharply up at me. 'Now for goodness' sake, don't start to cry on me.'

I swallowed hard. My eyes were dripping and my nose was filling with snot. What a sight I must have looked.

He said, 'I think we may have to cool it for a bit. Otherwise we're heading straight for disaster.'

'How?'

'I told you, we're not playing games here. What I – and therefore you as well – stand to lose, is considerable. Now, I'm suggesting we draw back from the brink, just for a while.'

I said, 'You've stopped loving me.'

'That just shows how immature you really are, that you can even think that. It's because I care about you that I'm saying this.'

The door opened. Silly, innocent Miss Ridgeway came in. 'My, you both look very conspiratorial,' she said.

He answered without a shake in his voice: 'This foolish young lady has just managed to lose a chunk of her coursework. We're trying to work out what to do.'

'Oh, poor you! Was it handwritten or on the computer?'

'Er... handwritten,' I muttered.

'Oh dear, then you don't have a copy. What was it in? Was it in a file?'

I fumbled around for words. 'It was . . . er . . . a black ring binder.'

'And when did you last see it?'

'I don't know. I'm afraid I may have left it on the bus.'

'Oh, my dear! Have you tried lost property? I know my friend Margaret left her handbag on the bus with all her money in it, and would you believe it someone actually handed it in! So you should give them a ring.'

'Thanks. I will.'

'Now, what was it I came to tell you? Ah yes. Geoffrey, just to let you know that you don't need to cover for Sally this afternoon; Mrs Mason has said she'll do it herself. I do hope that coursework turns up, Hannah.' She turns to go, and I feel I have to go after her. But before I do, I look at him. He's looking up at me, and he's smiling, ruefully. I'm glad of that, at least. But I still feel terrible.

**Friday 14th December**

My marks are getting so bad. You have exams next term, Hannah, everyone keeps saying. Don't I know. Oh I wish everything would stop.

I've put on half a pound this week. I must stop pigging. There has to be something I get right.

I should start thinking about Christmas shopping. I've usually done it by now. But I feel so exhausted.

**Sunday 16th December**

Grace is getting hysterical about the wedding. Half the people haven't replied to the invitations and they need to sort out the catering. She was here on Sunday, and we had one wedding drama after another. At least the good thing was that nobody took any notice of me. I was able to leave half the food that Mum had insisted on piling up on my plate, and no one seemed to see.

I don't feel hungry any more, so I think I'm getting that right, at last. I ought to go jogging, or something; then I'd really start to lose more quickly. But I'm so tired, I can hardly drag myself around.

**Monday 17th December**

I feel quite empty inside my head, not even unhappy. Everything's just going thud, thud, thud. I can't see any point in anything. When I look back on that carefree silly girl I was, this summer even!

If I had been more sensible, it wouldn't have come to this, I know it. He's scared of me now, because he can't trust me. And you can't really blame him.

Oh, you fool, Hannah, you fool!

And we break up on Wednesday. How can I get through Christmas without even a word from him. And I know there isn't going to be one.

# Chapter Thirteen

**Tuesday 18th December**

He can't let the term end without *something* – I know he can't. I kept going over the scene when I was in bed last night. He brushes past me in the corridor. Without a word he slips something into my hand as he passes. For a second his hand closes over mine, and he squeezes it ever so gently. I tighten my grip over a screw of tissue paper and as soon as I can, go to the cloakroom and lock myself in a toilet so that I can see his gift. There on my palm I see it glittering – what? At first I imagine a ring, but I don't think he'd give me a ring – rings have too many connotations and I don't think we're at that point yet. Maybe it's a silver heart on a silver chain – I've always despised those for being naff, but if *he* had given it to me…For a while I think about how I'm going to get away with wearing it. Mum is bound to notice, but I could tell her it's from Tasha. Or even, I bought it for myself. I find myself worrying about this bit of the story. And then I realise – how stupid. He hasn't given me anything, yet.

I should have got something for him. But I don't think I can, just at the moment. He'd have to hide it, or make up a story about it. And he's so cross with me that I don't want to give him that extra hassle.

But to think we'll be celebrating Christmas away from each other. The time when you want to be with the people you love, and I can't even mention his name.

Mum is now in full Christmas swing. I don't know how she does it. The wreath on the front door has arrived from that smart flower shop and the Christmas tree is coming tomorrow. She's unpacked the decorations and Maria is polishing up the silver, ironing the linen and cleaning the crystal. Plus there's the drinks party for the neighbours on the 23rd and Grandmother and Grandfather who'll come from Oxford on Christmas Eve and Granny Bennett down from Yorkshire. Felix comes tomorrow, and Grace, Daniel and Daniel's parents will arrive on the day. The little kids from the local school will be singing carols on the corner, and Mum will go round as she always does with mince pies, which she buys in industrial quantities. Then on Christmas Eve, it'll be Midnight Mass and more carols . . .

I remember how I used to lie awake on Christmas Eve, just so full of excitement. I used to think, I cannot bear this, I just cannot bear to wait until tomorrow. But I always had to. And now, what am I going to be thinking?

Tasha tells me I don't look well. Someone else says that too. Have I stopped eating or something? I wish.

Tim Wilmot's having a party. Tasha's going. But I shall make some excuse. There's a party at Zoë's too, on Friday. But Nat will probably be there, so I certainly shan't turn up for that.

I don't feel in the party mood, anyway.

I didn't even see him today, except briefly at a distance. But maybe he'll find time for a word tomorrow. I can't imagine he'll let us part without a word, not at Christmas of all times.

**Wednesday 19th December**

It's over. School is over. And he never said anything.

It was the usual last-day noise, kisses and Christmas cards and presents.

I didn't give any cards this year. Said I'd been too busy. I didn't want any either, but I got some back.

Across the corridor, just for a moment, and he even avoided my gaze! I can't bear it.

On the way home, I got the bus to Ken High Street. I was feeling sick but I thought I ought to get at least Mum and Dad's presents.

I was on the bus. I was going to get off at the station.

And then, I looked across the road. She was *there*. Dressed in a dark coat, with a bright pink scarf flung around her shoulders. She looked so well, so happy. She was coming out of that road by the library. She turned as if she was talking to someone behind her, and then she spun round again, still laughing. She seemed to give off light and happiness. People turned to look at her.

And then she looked up at the bus where I was sitting and for a second our eyes met.

And I saw her scorn, and her hatred. *Not long now*, she seemed to be saying, *not long now*.

I'm so scared.

**Thursday 20th December**

A day on which I know there's simply no chance of seeing him – no chance at all. Because he'll be being all lovey-dovey in Acton with Jenny and the two children, won't he? They'll have him all to themselves.

Felix came home yesterday, sarcastic as ever.

The house is filling up with food. It's so gross. I don't know how I'm going to manage – nothing but eating going on all around me for days and days. Food everywhere – the house smelling of it, the kitchen heaped with it. Meal after meal after meal, at which I've got to smile, and eat, and smile. I don't how I shall bear it, quite frankly.

Mum sent me round the Square to hand deliver some cards she'd forgotten. A safe little job for our Hannah. It was cold and misty – only three o'clock in the afternoon, but people already had their lights on, and the car tyres swooshed on the wet roads. Swathes of golden decorations everywhere – great trees lit up and holly wreaths on the doors.

And then I saw a taxi draw up, just over the road. The driver got out laughing, and opened the door. Obviously a very *special* passenger.

And there she was, her cheeks pink and healthy in the cold air, her eyes shining.

She was laden with bags and parcels, gift-wrapped packages poking out everywhere. Her arms could hardly manage them, she was so laden. She and the taxi driver laughed as she fumbled for her change…

She's getting closer...

**Friday 21st December**

A card fell on the mat for me in grown-up handwriting, and I thought, he's remembered!

But it was only from my old piano teacher.

Ruthie is being such a pain with her endless, you'll never guess what I've got you!

I've got to do something. But I'm scared to go to the High Street in case she's there. I feel sick, and hopeless, and afraid.

**Saturday 22nd December**

My last chance to do my Christmas shopping. Why can't I move? All this activity going on around me, and I feel stranded like a whale. Even though I don't eat, I'm so so disgustingly fat. I can clutch rolls of it in my hands, around my waist, my thighs, my bum.

I wonder what he's doing now? I can see him hanging up the decorations in that little front room of his, while Jenny is rushing around busily and the son and the daughter are arguing and wrapping presents and phoning their friends.

Tash phoned to say the party was great. I don't care.

I'm sure I saw *her* again from the window, waiting in the misty trees, in the Square. Biding her time.

**Later**

I still haven't gone out and soon it's going to be too late.

Everyone rushing around like mad things.

What will they say when they find out?

And then, I think, it doesn't matter, does it? She's got them everything in those parcels.

Does she want him as well? I guess he'd like her better than me, anyway.

It's getting dark. If I go out now, if I cut through the park, I could still make it to the shops…

# Chapter Fourteen

And there your diary comes to an end. Just suddenly, just like that.

I feel lost, let down, stood up.

You were in such a strange mood that day. Did you do your shopping? How can you not have got presents for your family? Even I, hopeless male that I am, manage to get some sort of Christmas shopping done in time – last year, I got Mum one of those cheap scarves that pretends to be expensive, and for Cara some posh bath stuff she'd been banging on about endlessly.

We had a pretty good Christmas last year, though obviously it wasn't a patch on yours. No silver to polish or crystal to clean. No wreath on the door, because if you put one on the door round here, someone would nick it within five seconds. No mounds of food or mince pies for grateful carol singers. Mum usually does a last minute dash to Marks in the hope that they'll be selling off things cheap by the time she arrives. (One year she did that, she was too late for anything except two packets of chili-flavoured chicken thighs, so we had those for our Christmas lunch.) Gran came over from Hainault, with Great-Gran in tow. Great-Gran insisted on having the telly up so loud that we couldn't hear ourselves think, then fell asleep in the chair and snored and farted all afternoon. On Boxing Day, I went up to Dad's in Birmingham. Cara spent the day with her mum no doubt calling up spirits from the grave and aligning pyramids with Tutankhamun's tomb, or whatever it is she does. Cara had to go to her dad's on Boxing Day too – she was a bit pissed off over this as her stepmother's a mad born-again Christian. But we both like our dads, though we don't see much of them. I can't imagine having a dad like yours, who barely seems to notice his family and whom everyone steps around as though he's so special. Even when he's only talking to me on the phone, Dad can suss out if I'm worried or distracted.

So he should. That's what dads are for, isn't it?

I wonder too, like you obviously did, about Mr Creep, having a jolly time with his little family. Did he think about you? Or did he think, phew, got away with it again that time! It was a close-run thing though!

And I have disturbing memories too, of that Christmas. Of stories in the local paper, and police tape in the park . . .

No. Shut up, Tom.

The thing now, is what am I going to do with this poxy diary? Left it far too late to share it with anyone now.

The thing is, Hannah, you seem to have become part of my life. I've known you like you never get to know a girl, or even another person. You've told your diary things you'd never tell anyone, and now they're part of me, too . . .

*

I keep thinking of her, and yet I don't even know if I'd like her. She's so different from me, with her posh house and her assumption that everyone else lives in posh houses too. She'd probably think I was dead common.

I'd probably think she was a total snob, not the sort of girl I'd look at twice normally. No, that's not true. I expect I would look at her. She may not be at all like I imagine her – a pale face, great dark eyes and a sort of cloud of dark hair all around her face – that's just the picture I have. But I bet she's a babe. After all, whatever she might want to think, it isn't her *beautiful mind* that Mr Creep fell for, is it?

And then I think, wait a moment. After all this diary is just words on a page, pages in a book, isn't it? How do I know any of it's true? Maybe it's just someone who can write a good story, winding me up. Maybe there's no Hannah, no Mr Creep, no rich, chilly family, no big house. It's all a joke to someone . . .

But I don't want to believe that. It's become too real to me. I have to trust it. Some things can't be faked. That although she didn't especially have me in mind – how could she have done? – she wanted to tell someone. It was important that someone listen and know what she had been going through. I just don't feel anyone could have made it up, not like this . . . You have to go with your feelings sometimes.

Still, the problem remains: what am I going to do with this diary? I can't keep it. I don't want to throw it away.

It shouldn't end up on a skip again. But now, I really don't want to show it to Mum or Cara. Sorry, but I just don't.

What I really want to do is to take it back to Hannah. Find out why she threw it away.

If it was Hannah who threw it away...And that's another problem altogether...

I've got to find Hannah. Somehow I've got to find her.

# Chapter Fifteen

And I have no idea how I'm going to do this. After all, she's left so few clues about herself. I don't know her address, or even her surname. I don't know which school she goes to. I'm amazed she could have written so many pages without even dropping these simple clues.

But I'm going to have to find out somehow. I'll have to go through the diary like some stupid Sherlock Holmes.

Hell. If I felt like a creep the first time reading it through, I'm going to feel a real slithery slimy worm this time. I'm going to have to turn myself into Hannah's stalker.

But I can live with that. After all, stalkers are usually up to no good. All I want to do is to find out if Hannah's still all right and give her back what belongs to her. I don't see how trying to find her can do any harm.

So I assemble my detective kit. It's not very complicated – just an A4 pad with the doodled-on pages torn off and a biro. I have to make a list of the few bits of information I can glean about Hannah, in the hope that they'll lead me to her.

Hannah ????? Age – probably 16 or 17. Probably in lower sixth form. Goes to posh girls' private school somewhere. History teacher at school: Miss Ridgeway. English teacher: Geoffrey Sinclair. GS married to Jenny Sinclair, has two children. Lives in Acton.

Hannah has brother Felix. Sisters Grace and Ruthie. Grace is going to marry some Indian bloke. Mother runs some sort of company, is demon cook etc. Father doesn't say much but is brilliant. I have no idea what he does, except he's a Catholic.

I don't know her address either, but it's a big house, somewhere near Holland Park. Well, that should narrow it down to a mere few hundred locations, shouldn't it?

We're having a day off school – one of those days I used to think were called Insect Days when I was a little kid. I'm alone in the house. Cara had her own plans for today. I said I'd do my revision, then just crash out on the sofa and watch a few videos.

If only. This is doing my head in. There must be something here, in all these pages. What is it I know most about?

What about the school? I remember this moment in the last year of primary school when, though we'd all been pretty much equal in the past, we all suddenly divided into two camps – there were the kids frantically having private tuition and doing entrance exams, and the rest of us just having to take our chances with the local comp.

Well, that was fine by me. Though there are some real scumbags in our school, I'm glad I went. Wouldn't have met Cara otherwise, and I've got some good friends there too. Besides, those kids used to get so worked up about their exams and so gutted if they didn't pass. Plus all these pushy parents egging them on.

But I remember the names of most of the schools that they were going for. My girlfriend at the time (Ah! And I've never seen her since then!) was called Holly, and she was taking several exams. Got into her second choice, in the end.

There actually weren't that many schools. I write down a few names. Then I remember something. Sir took her on a little jaunt to Chiswick, didn't he, and it didn't sound as though he was taking her too far away.

I have an idea. It's a bit devious and I'm not usually devious. But it just might work.

I get the map and tick off the private girls' schools which aren't that far from Chiswick. I end up with a list of four. The Yellow Pages gives me numbers for all of them. I phone up the first on the list. A secretary answers. She doesn't sound very friendly. I've planned what I'm going to say. The conversation goes like this.

Me: 'Excuse me, I wonder if you would let me have an address for Mr Sinclair. He used to be my sister's teacher, only she's in America and she's asked me to try to get in touch with him.'

Her: 'Mr Sinclair? There's no Mr Sinclair here.'

Me: 'Oh. I'm sorry. I must have got the wrong information somewhere.'

At the second school the conversation goes much the same, except that this time she's a really friendly old dear, who's ever so sorry she can't help me.

Well, this is what I expected. I've even got a default conversation ready just in case I'm put through to a staff room and Mr S in person is standing there. ('Oh, hallo, Sir, actually it was a pupil of yours I needed to contact urgently, only it's a bit embarrassing.' I imagine he would be pretty embarrassed. I would be too, so I'm glad this didn't happen.)

Then I pick up the phone and dial the number for The Lady Collier Girls' High School. That was Holly's first choice I remember, the one she didn't get into. I remember her saying mournfully, 'Mummy says only really clever girls get into Lady Collier's.')

This time, when I've said my spiel, there's a silence at the other end of the line. Then the voice – posh, pained – comes back at me. 'I'm afraid we can't give out the addresses of staff over the phone. No school would be prepared to do that for you. What was it concerning, do you know?'

'I don't know, I'm afraid, my sister wanted to get in touch.'

'Well, all I can suggest, dear, is that you direct your letter here and we'll see that it's passed on to Mr Sinclair. Do you know our postcode?'

My hand is shaking as I put down the phone. I have absolutely no intention of writing to Mr Creep, of course. But I've found out what school he teaches at. His school. And Hannah's.

So what now? No one from Lady Collier's is going to

supply your friendly neighbourhood stalker with a list of names and address of pupils, are they? But now I've got this one little bit of crucial information, perhaps I can use it as a lever to find out some more. Suddenly I'm feeling optimistically close.

# Chapter Sixteen

I hadn't made any more plans, after this. But as I sit there, mulling things over, I get impatient. Just want to be doing something. Though I'm not sure what.

So I get out our A-Z and work out where Lady Collier's is. A bus ride or two stops on the Tube should do it. It's not a bit of London I know well, but it's near Hammersmith and the road Mum and I take when we're going westwards out of London.

I take my school bag, tip all the junk out on the bed, and instead put in Hannah's diary, my A4 pad and a biro, and the London map.

It's half past two when I leave. I have to wait fifteen minutes for the bus, and it crawls a bit through Shepherd's Bush and Olympia. I get off at Hammersmith, and dive off through the shopping centre and away into quieter streets of Victorian houses. It's now about three-fifteen. The street opens out into a square – big houses on three sides, and on the fourth, behind an ornamental railing, I see The Lady Collier School. A big green sign announces this in gold letters. There's a long, low modern building and a more ornamental red brick one, which might be Victorian. It's not especially interesting as a building, but then it doesn't need to be,

I guess. All the parents who need to know, know that like my little friend Holly said, only the really clever girls get in to Lady Collier's.

I'm sorry now that she didn't. Could have met her here, and maybe found out a few things that I wanted to know. Plus, she was really quite cute, was Holly. A pity we lost touch. Anyway. Past history now. Let's concentrate on the issue in hand.

There doesn't seem to be anyone about. I don't know what time the school day finishes here, but it's probably a little early. I don't want to be spotted hanging about, so I go for a wander around some of the local streets. Ten minutes feels a lot when you're just trying to kill time.

Anyway, it's now nearer three-thirty. I've guessed the school day might finish now, and it seems I'm right. From where I am, I can hear a bell sounding and a ripple of sound coming up from the open windows of the modern building. It's not long before doors start to open and girls come rushing out. I stand hunched by the gate trying not to look like a drug dealer or some other lowlife. There are a few other people by the gates, a couple of mums, and a guy on a motorbike who might be someone's boyfriend. I don't feel so conspicuous now.

There's a surge of younger girls. They wear a hideous green and yellow uniform. Poor Hannah, I think. Then some older girls, wearing normal clothes. I imagine sixth formers don't have to wear the green-and-yellow rubbish. I imagine Cara would have a fit if anyone tried to put her into all of that.

I miss Cara now. I wish I'd confided in her. All of this would be much more normal if I had Cara with me. It would be quite natural for us to be following up these things together. As it is . . . I feel weird and a bit grubby.

I've worked out a sort of plan, while I've been standing here. I scan the girls coming out, and I target my three. They're wearing their own clothes so I assume they're sixth formers. They're all quite pretty, and they're having a good giggle over something, which is why I think they might be approachable.

They swing out of the school gate, and on to the pavement, hunched up very close to each other still jabbering away.

'Excuse me,' I say.

All three stop talking, and look me up and down, sizing me up. I feel like a slave in a slave market. But I have my fibbing story ready. I'm getting rather worryingly good at this.

'I'm looking for a girl called Hannah? I don't know her, but my brother? He's got this kind of crush on her? Only he's too shy? He's asked me to give her a message?' I feel a right dork, but they fall about giggling even more as if they believe me.

'Too shy, is he?'

'Ah, diddums!'

'Bless!'

'Sophie's good with shy boys, aren't you, Soph?'

'I thought shy was your speciality, Lou.'

Well, it doesn't seem that any of this lot are my Hannah. But we're getting off the point a bit here.

'Do you know Hannah?'

'Hannah who?'

'There's lots of Hannahs,' one explains patiently. 'Do you know what year she's in?'

'The sixth form, I guess.'

'Higher or Intermediate?'

I gawp, but one of them intervenes patronisingly to explain their school's secret language to this comprehensive lout. 'Upper or Lower, to you.'

Roll on the revolution, I think to myself. But I reply with what's meant to be a charming smile. 'Lower, I think. I'm not quite sure.'

'Well we've got three Hannahs in first year sixth. Which one do you want?'

'I don't know. My brother doesn't know her surname.'

'Well, there's Hannah Green, Hannah Levine or Hannah Townsend.'

I shrug. 'I don't know. He said she was gorgeous though.'

'Hannah Levine!' say the girls and collapse with hysterics. 'She's so-o-o gorgeous!' They're saying it in a sarcastic way which implies that poor Hannah Levine is anything but gorgeous. 'Someone somewhere must fancy Hannah Levine!' they say, rubbing the point home.

Hannah Green, Hannah Levine, Hannah Townsend. I've got to keep these names in my head.

But one of my girls has spotted something in the distance. 'There's Daddy's car! Come on, Soph, want a lift? Lou?' And they dive off. The one called Soph calls back to me, 'Remember if your brother wants a cure for his shyness, just pass him on to Lou!'

'No, Sophie! Tell him Sophie's the name!'

And they've gone.

Well. I've found three Hannahs. The girls didn't seem to think there was anything odd in the request. Which deals with one of my anxieties. Because if anything horrible had happened to a Hannah recently, they wouldn't be standing here giggling, would they?

Mustn't forget those three names, though. I take out my pad and scribble them down: Green, Levine, Townsend. Makes a little rhyme almost. Quite easy to remember.

And then when I'm wondering what to do next, I see a man coming out of the main door. He's surrounded by four girls, who are jumping up and down and laughing around him. He's smiling back at them. He wears a dark corduroy jacket, and is carrying a pile of books. He's not very tall, has darkish hair, just beginning to go at the temples, and dark eyes. He has a big nose and a silly grin. He's not the sort of person you'd look at twice normally. A bit of a nerd, you'd think. But it's the way he's talking to those girls that makes me look.

If a bloke who taught at our school went around surrounded by adoring girls like that, someone would say something.

They smile and bob up and down around him, and he bends his head and smiles back. He touches one on the shoulder to emphasise a point.

If a bloke who taught at my school was behaving that way with a group of girls, you'd call it inappropriate behaviour. And at my school, that would be just not on.

Somehow I don't want to hang around any more. I turn and head off in the direction of the bus stop.

A silly little man with a big nose and a goofy grin. Who likes to be surrounded by adoring young girls. It seems to me that while I haven't found Hannah today, I've certainly found her Mr Sinclair.

# Chapter Seventeen

To be honest, I feel a bit disgusted with myself after this. As though I'm the one who's been up to no good. When I get home I dismantle my detective kit, stash Hannah's diary away in a drawer, and try to get on with my life. Which I do for a few days, quite normally.

But then in spite of myself, I start going over things again.

To begin with, there's her name. I think of the way the girls responded over poor Hannah Levine. I wonder what's wrong with her. Probably she's ugly, and I just don't think my Hannah is ugly. My Hannah's obsessed with her weight, though she's obviously quite thin. But even she doesn't seem to think she's ugly. Mr Sinclair wouldn't be interested in an ugly girl.

Then I keep thinking about him. Okay, so he's a nerd. Love is blind, but it's not supposed to be moronic as well. Hannah goes down a few notches in my estimation for her taste in men.

But maybe he really is a great teacher. Maybe he flatters her and makes her feel good. I don't know. Who can tell?

The more I think about it, though, the angrier I get on her behalf. Kids do get crushes on teachers, even in our school, occasionally. I had a crush on that sexy Science teacher when I was fourteen. Really fancied her. But if she'd suddenly turned round and said, 'Want a shag?' I reckon I'd have run a mile. She was just a fantasy woman, for me, for a while. Then I got over it. Sir should have behaved better with Hannah, no doubt about it.

I think about the way he treated her, how he managed to leave her feeling guilty, though he's the one who's behaved badly, right from the start. She's been swept along by him – almost can't help herself, I reckon. He gets to have sex with her. Then he tells her she's immature and stupid. Even what she says about his wife, which isn't smart, I admit it, is only when she's been pushed into a corner.

Mum has a cousin who reminds me of this behaviour. She always wants Mum's time and attention, and always makes Mum feel guilty and in the wrong. Did it even when they were children, Mum said. Won't let go, won't let you off the hook. Manipulative, Mum calls it. I reckon Mr Sinclair is the King of Manipulative. If only Hannah could see it . . .

Hannah. I try the names out. Hannah Levine. Probably not, not after what those girls said. Hannah Green. I like the sound of Hannah Green – has a good ring to it. I'm almost decided on this, when I work through the other names in the family, and I realise, no one, not even Hannah's fairly insensitive parents would christen their first child Grace Green!

So back to Hannah Townsend. While Mum's out at her night school, I flick through the local telephone directory. Trouble is, it's quite a common name. A whole column of them. No way of knowing which one's my Hannah.

But I'm back in Sherlock Holmes mode now. I pick out all the numbers with a W8 or W14 postcode. Still there are quite a few of them.

Then I remember something. Hannah mentions the 'Square' several times. Does she live in Something Square?

I look down the list again. And then I see it. 'D.J Townsend, 19 St Nicholas Square, W8.'

I think I've just found Hannah.

So now what? Actually, at this point I do what I did before and chicken out for a few days. After all, I can't really turn up on Hannah's doorstep in posh St Nicholas Square and tell her I disapprove of her love life, can I?

I take a short cut through St Nicholas Square on my way to school sometimes. It really is serious money – huge houses set back on a hill, a private garden in the middle, and a Victorian church in one corner.At this time of year the front gardens are a mass of cherry blossom, cascading shrubs and billowing flowers. I suppose you could live in one of those houses and think that the rest of the world lives that way, but it really doesn't. Maybe Hannah needed to come down to earth a bit, maybe meeting Mr Sinclair in his 'little house' wasn't a bad thing . . .

No. That's not true. Meeting Mr Sinclair was a very bad thing for her. But I imagine from the way things were going before Christmas that it's all over by now. And what sort of a state will that leave Hannah in?

Yet, if Hannah Townsend is 'my' Hannah, then the girls outside the school didn't talk about her as though there was any reason why my imaginary brother shouldn't have had a crush on her. They didn't say, She's been ill, or she's in a bad way, or she's not been at school for a bit . . .

But then I remember something else. The other thing that Hannah was talking about in her diary. At first I didn't take much notice of it, thought she was imagining it. Then there was what Cara's mum had said that day in Norfolk. I'd worried about that for a bit. Then I got so involved with wondering where the Mr Sinclair business was heading that I didn't think about the other stuff.

But Hannah was worried all right. And even though she was obviously getting paranoid about her weight, and even though she'd made a huge error of judgement in her love life, she didn't strike me as a girl who would imagine things. She feared the girl she kept seeing, on the street or in doorways, the girl who seemed to get prettier and healthier as Hannah became more and more unhappy and sick . . .

I've been thinking this over and over, since last night. And I can't sit here any more. It's Saturday morning, and I'm supposed to be meeting Cara later on. I've got an hour or so, though.

I call out a goodbye to Mum, and rush out, just as I am. Hannah's diary is still locked away in my drawer. I want to leave it there, for a bit.

I set off, out of our estate, down Ladbroke Grove, into Holland Park Avenue, the usual way I go to school. The houses get larger and grander by the minute. It's a beautiful spring day today. The sun is out and the houses look clean and golden. There's a dazzle of blossom and flowers everywhere. People are taking off their jackets. They're starting to wear warm weather colours – pale pinks and light greens and creams.

I turn off the main road and enter St Nicholas Square. A man is trimming his hedge and gives me a dirty look as I pass. Hell, they probably even have their own security guards here in this square. It must be worth the gross national income of a small African country, if you added it all up.

Other than the man in his garden, the square is empty. I find number nineteen. As big as all the others, white painted door, slightly clinical garden full of clipped shrubs, some jaunty red tulips in a window box.

And then, as if on cue, the front door opens.

A girl comes out. She's turning to finish her conversation with someone in the house. I hear her say, 'Don't worry! I won't! Love you lots!'

She turns, still laughing from the conversation she's been having and comes tripping down the path.

She's about sixteen or seventeen. She's wearing a summery dress with a cardigan flung over it – the dress is pink, clingy and embroidered with tiny flowers. The cardigan is deeper pink with a little ruffle at the neck. She's wearing strappy sandals, and no tights. Though her legs are pale, they look good. She isn't that tall, maybe not quite as tall as I imagined. She's thin and delicate, but not at all like a skeleton. You could pinch those arms and find them soft and cushiony.

And her face. It isn't quite the Hannah I imagined, but she's certainly gorgeous. She's dark – I was right about that, but her hair has a chestnut tint to it, and it billows around her face in a pre-Raphaelite sort of way. Her face is pale, and her eyes are big and dark – hazel or dark blue, I can't quite see from here.

She seems quite confident and at ease in her skin as she bounds down the path. Not someone you can imagine agonising over whether people love her, or whether she's too fat...

I wonder if anyone in her family would notice if one day she suddenly changed, seemed to be a different person, a person who was happier, more easy going, more carefree, than she'd been just the day before...

Maybe they would notice and they'd just feel relieved about it. I don't know.

I find myself going up to the gate. I get there just as she clangs it open. She looks at me. Our eyes meet. She's like a princess, slightly haughty, amused and yet gracious and glamorous all at once.

'Hannah?'
'Who wants to know?'
'Hannah,' I say, 'I found your diary.'